I0663124

A HARDY DAY'S WORK

The girl was beautiful and blonde and clearly worried. "Please, Mr. Hardy, I need your help."

"Well . . ." said Hardy, pouring her a drink.

"Please, Mr. Hardy. Sit with me. Even if you can't help me, I must tell someone."

Hardy went to the couch. "What seems to be the trouble?"

"You must help me in buying back some photographs. If my husband ever sees them, he will kill me."

"And what do those photographs prove?" asked Hardy, watching her firm braless breasts rise and fall in agitation beneath the thin material of her sweater.

She licked her lips and pulled him down on the couch. "That I am a nymphomaniac."

It was then that Hardy knew he wouldn't be able to stop until he got to the bottom of this case . . . even though he might be digging his own grave . . .

Books by Martin Meyers

Patrick Hardy Mysteries

Kiss and Kill
Spy and Die
Red is for Murder
Hung up to Die
Reunion for Death

Dutchman Historical Mysteries
by Annette Meyers and Martin Meyers,
Writing as Maan Meyers

The Kingsbridge Plot
The High Constable
The House on Mulberry Street
The Lucifer Contract
The Organ Grinder
The Dutchman
The Dutchman's Dilemma

Visit us at www.speakingvolumes.us

HARDY

KISS AND KILL

Martin Meyers

SPEAKING VOLUMES, LLC
NAPLES, FLORIDA
2016

HARDY
KISS AND KILL

Copyright © 1975 Martin Meyers

All rights reserved. No part of this book may be reproduced
or transmitted in any form or by any means without written
permission of the author.

ISBN 978-1-62815-357-6

For more exciting
Books, eBooks, Audiobooks and more visit us at
www.speakingvolumes.us

Chapter One

The fat man walked into the barber shop just as the killer placed the gun to the toweled head of the man in the chair. The fat man wanted to turn and run but he couldn't.

"No, don't," he shouted.

The man without a face pulled the trigger and the man in the chair was dead. The fat man still couldn't move. His eyes were riveted on the bloody mess that used to be a head.

"Tough luck, Fatso."

The fat man looked away from the mess in the chair in time to look into the eyes of the killer as he shot him in the stomach.

"Oh my God!"

He fell to the floor, clutching his large middle.

"Oh God, please don't let me die." He screamed it again and again. "Oh God, please don't let me die."

At last. The nightmare was over. Patrick Hardy pulled off his pajama top. It was soaked. He walked

5

into the bathroom and splashed his face and chest with cold water. As he wiped the water away he looked at himself in the mirror. No matter how often he did it, it was like looking at a stranger. The firm chin, the well-developed body, marred only by the pucker of scar tissue on his stomach. That wasn't the Pat Hardy he knew. He talked to himself in the mirror.

"What ever happened to fat old lovable Pat Hardy?"

He didn't wait for an answer. He knew. He lay down on the bed again, lit a cigarette and thought back to the barber shop.

Once every two months young Patrick Hardy would get off his fat rear and waddle over to the shop for a haircut and a beard trim. His was a happy existence. Because of his father's money he was able to enjoy his sedentary life with his books and his food and his television. This was a busy day for him. After his haircut he was due at the draft board. An inconvenience but no menace. His 325 pounds would disqualify him for anyone's army. Life was good. The sun was shining. The walk from Riverside Drive had not been too tiring, and he was looking forward to his dinner of veal and cream sauce, his new book and an evening of television.

He walked into the barber shop.

They dug three bullets out of him that night, all from his ample stomach. His extra layers of fat probably kept a slug from reaching anything vital, but they certainly didn't make the surgeon's job any easier. A fourth shot had caught him in the knee. By morning the bullets had been removed, and he was in a coma. He stayed comatose for more than two weeks, existing solely on intravenous injections. When he came out of it, his prognosis was good. The only aftereffect, besides a trick knee and several scars, was the loss of ninety pounds. Hardy was sure he could remedy that in a short time.

While he convalesced the police kept visiting him with pictures to look at and questions to answer. He couldn't help them. He couldn't remember the killer's face. The case was finally considered just another unsolved gangland killing.

Hardy had problems of his own. None of his clothes fit. To his surprise his weight stayed around 235 pounds. When he was fit enough to visit his draft board again, they were surprised too. So much so that they changed his classification and drafted him. (They didn't believe him about the trick knee.)

As he lay there in his sweaty bed, he couldn't decide which memory was more horrifying: the day he got shot, or the day he got drafted. He lit another cigarette and thought about the camp they sent him to after he was processed. He thought about the camp and the speech that the gung-ho lieutenant made to the new men.

"My name is Lieutenant Norden. It is my misfortune to be your commanding officer. I have met some foul-ups and rejects in my day, but you men win the prize. And that is exactly why you are here. If each of you goof-ups looks around you, you will find that you are all of a kind. They tell me you're all geniuses—150 I.Q. and all that. You're also too fat, you're too skinny, you're too weak, and you're scared. Each of you is a grade A coward. Well, your Uncle Sam is going to try an experiment . . . and you are going to be the guinea pigs. We people are going to make fighting men out of you people even if it kills you."

7

Hardy was marched and trained and drilled. They trimmed the rest of the fat off him and got him in shape, but he was still a rotten soldier. Then they played their ace. Using the Pavlovian Theory of Conditioned Reflex, they brainwashed him into re-acting aggressively when danger threatened. It worked. He was still a coward, but a fighting coward. He could be as frightened as he wanted to be, but if someone attacked, his body would ignore the command of his brain to run. His reflexes would take over, and he would defend and counterattack . . . only then would he get scared.

Pat's little unit was shipped to the East. The men were found to be very effective in actual combat, but they all reverted to type between engagements and became a scared mob. More than half of the group went over the hill at the prospect of further danger. Not Hardy, he was too scared even to do that. The Government gave the project up as a lost cause and scrapped the whole thing as impractical. They rounded up the AWOLs and loaded the entire unit into a truck that was to take them to a plane bound for Tokyo. The truck hit a mine and killed everyone but Patrick Hardy, who survived without a scratch.

He lay there in his sweat thinking about it. He thought about it a lot. The army let him serve out the rest of his time in Europe. Not knowing what to do with Hardy, they assigned him to an M.P. outfit where he warmed a chair and pushed papers around. When his hitch was up he was separated in Paris. He made a discovery there: after the army had slimmed him down and trimmed him up, he found he was attractive to women—very attractive. So, at 25, Patrick Hardy discovered sex . . . and he liked it. He still loved food and the easy life, but he didn't want to give up his

8

new appetite. So he compromised. He still gourmandised and loafed, but each day, and much to his regret, he worked out. His whole life was dedicated to his two appetites: sex and food. He was a satyr and a glutton. This thin man with the soul of a fat man was also an automatic, if unwilling, fighting machine.

Chapter Two

When morning came it was accompanied by rain. April in Paris. What a liar that songwriter was. Hardy quickly went through his exercises. He made them more bearable by thinking of breakfast and Simone. Simone was a dancer he had met the week before. Nothing had happened then, but promises had been made, and he expected fulfillment this afternoon. He enjoyed his breakfast, but he never did have a chance to enjoy Simone.

After breakfast the concierge handed him a telegram. "Regret to inform you that your father died in his sleep this morning."

It was signed by some lawyer. Hardy caught the next plane back to the U.S. He sincerely mourned for his father, but human nature being what it is, especially his human nature, his thoughts turned to the money. His father had been a rich man. As it turned out, "had been" was right. When Hardy got to New York he found that his entire legacy consisted of an apartment on Riverside Drive, a year-old Volkswagen, two thousand dollars and his father's best wishes.

Thankfully, the apartment had a good kitchen. While he ate his own version of steak Diane he considered his two major problems—women and money.

The women weren't really a problem. Within the next few months he met quite a few. But the money was soon gone. And, though it was offered, Hardy couldn't take money from women. He was tempted, but he couldn't. So he had to find a way of making a living.

He didn't like fancy dinner parties as a rule, but Jennifer Burns had a good cook, Jennifer Burns was also very beautiful and . . . after dinner? . . . when the other guests had gone? . . . One never knew. As a matter of fact, he didn't like parties of any sort. He didn't like much of anything that caused him to leave his apartment. If he had his way he would stock up on food, books and women and never go outdoors. But the world wasn't like that. So, if he wanted Jennifer Burns' food, and if he wanted Jennifer Burns . . . ? He went to the party.

Dinner conversations with strangers always bored him. They were always the same. A little soup and then a question. A bite of bread and then a comment. A sip of wine and another question. On and on and on, till mercifully the coffee was served. And, always the same questions. "Where are you from, Mr. Hardy? What do you do?" Sometimes he was a brain surgeon, other times he was an ex-priest. Tonight he was a detective.

"A detective? What a marvelous coincidence. I happen to be in need of a detective. May I have your number?"

Reluctantly, he gave it to the woman next to him

and forgot all about it as he turned his attention to Jennifer Burns' lovely bosom as she leaned over to offer him some brandy.

"What's all this nonsense about your being a detective?" Jennifer asked later, as she stretched across the bed to get a cigarette.

"Light me one too," he said, and he looked at the different lovely parts of her body. "Oh, you mean what I said to that old talking machine you put me next to. Nothing to it. I just said it to shut her up!"

"That old talking machine happens to be Mrs. Emily Sidney, a very rich lady who happened to believe you, and she's going to call you tomorrow about a case."

He thought about it for a minute.

"Why not? All right, I'm a detective. Now put out that cigarette and come here."

Mrs. Sidney never did call him, but it didn't matter. He became a detective. He never thought of it as a violent occupation. He knew private detectives never handled murder and such. That was strictly paperback stuff. As far as he was concerned, private detectives followed people, found things and filled out reports. So he went through the proper paper work and applied for a license. He had cards printed up and inserted a small ad in the *Times* announcing that Patrick Hardy, Chief Consultant of TROUBLE LIMITED, was opening an office at 7 Riverside Drive. Business was surprisingly good and surprisingly easy. He traced stolen pets. He caught sticky-fingered cashiers. He followed husbands for wives and wives for husbands. It wasn't a brilliant career, but it was a living. It helped him to pay the rent and buy gas for the VW and eat almost the way he wanted to. And, of course, he met a lot of women in his new line of work. Jennifer married a Brazilian millionaire, but that was life.

12

Chapter Three

Sherlock Holmes came into Hardy's room and glowered at him. When that didn't work, he jumped up onto the bed and licked Hardy's face. Holmes was a black standard poodle that had been Jennifer's parting gift to Hardy.

"All right, Holmes. I'm getting up. All right."

Hardy read a little bit of *archie & mehitabel* to help make the transition between sleeping and waking, then he drank a glass of juice and tried to think of a good reason to skip his morning workout. He couldn't think of any, so he went into the small gym next to his bedroom and got it over with. After his shower his day really began. He had breakfast.

The apartment was on the ground floor and had a separate entrance from the rest of the building, away from the doorman and elevators and people. It was really two apartments combined. Hardy had taken a room of one and converted it into an office. After breakfast he went into the office and turned on the

13

radio. Ignoring the chair at his desk, he flopped down on the oversized black and brown velvet chaise next to it. With the sounds of WPAT for background, he started rereading *Swann's Way*.

At twelve thirty a newscaster told about all the trouble the world was in. Some of that trouble was fatal to a young girl who lived just a few blocks away from Hardy. While he went into the kitchen to get a dish of caponata he heard how Dorothy Robbins had been strangled to death the night before. The private detective shook his head at the thought of violence and went back to his book until an old Randolph Scott movie on TV took him away from the wonders of Proust. As he watched the hero tame the West, Hardy started preparing his dinner. At four-thirty the coq au vin was simmering and he settled down to watch another movie. Then the doorbell rang, and Holmes started barking. "I hear. I hear it."

He walked down the hall to open the front door and looked at his caller through the glass. It was very pleasant looking. She seemed young, not more than 25, and since Hardy was partial to statuesque brunettes, he was immediately partial to her. He opened the door.

"Patrick Hardy?"

"Speaking."

She stood there, fussing with her purse, apparently trying to decide how to phrase her next thought.

"Come on in," he told her.

"You are a detective, aren't you?"

"That's what I tell everyone. Don't be shy. Come on in. Holmes, stop barking. Relax, he won't bite. He's a big fake," said Hardy and he led her into the apartment.

Holmes came sniffing around while Hardy placed a

chair in front of his desk and turned off the TV.

"Holmes, stop that. Don't be fresh. I'd introduce you, but I don't know her name."

"Excuse me. I'm Peg Robbins."

"Holmes, meet Peg Robbins. Peg Robbins, meet . . . Oh . . . Any connection with Dorothy Robbins?"

"She's my . . . was my sister."

"I'm sorry," said Hardy. "Sit down, please. Would you like a drink?"

She shook her head and removed her dark glasses.

"Well, Miss Robbins. What can I do for you?"

"That's obvious. I want you to find my sister's murderer."

Hardy shook his head. "The police can do that a lot better than I can. And they won't send you a bill."

"Do you have a cigarette?"

As he sat down opposite her he gave her one and lit another for himself. She took a few nervous drags and then snuffed it out.

"I've just seen the police. They won't do anything. They're already blaming it on some unknown psychopath. I know better."

"What do you know?"

"I know my sister was killed by . . . the Organization."

"Look, Miss Robbins . . . Peg, I don't mean to make light of you. You've had a rough time and you're upset, but you've read too many detective novels. First, private detectives don't usually mess with murder. We're not equipped for it. Second, what do you mean, organization?"

"The mob. The people who run things. They probably run the police too."

Hardy sighed and leaned toward her.

"Before you say another word, read these." She

15

handed him three letters and took another cigarette from the pack on the desk. The letters were from Dorothy to Peg. They dealt mostly with what sisters write to sisters. She spoke about some men she dated and how her acting career was coming along. But each letter closed with remarks about her never realizing how evil the world could be, and how many evil men there were, and how these evil men were running things through their Organization. He put the letters in their envelopes and handed them back.

"Well?" she asked.

"Well what?"

"What she said."

"Where are you from?"

"Illinois."

"Chicago?"

"No. Down south, near Missouri. What's that got to do ... ?"

"Simple," he answered. "Any New Yorker knows by the time he's ten that the world is evil and that large parts of it are controlled by evil people. That's life. When you come from a small town in the Midwest ... It is a small town?"

"Population ten thousand."

"I thought so. Well, when you come from a place like that, even in this day of TV, you never believe that sort of thing until you see it for yourself. Your sister saw some of it. You can't miss seeing it in New York. Not that it doesn't exist anywhere else—it's just more blatant here."

She ground her cigarette out angrily. "You're just like all the rest. The Organization probably controls you too. If you won't help me, I'll find somebody who will."

"Hold your horses. I'd better help you. Otherwise

some crook will come along and take every cent you have. I'll only take some of it. Can you afford two hundred a day and expenses?"

She drew in a quick breath. "I'll take that drink now. Something sweet please. Yes, I can afford it."

He was surprised. He thought she'd refuse. The bar was behind him. Without getting up he poured a drink and handed it to her. "You sure?"

"Yes. Mother was very rich."

"That means your sister had money too."

"No, it doesn't."

She sipped the Cherry Heering. "Mother died when we were both young and left all the money to Daddy. When Dotty decided to be an actress Daddy disowned her. Daddy's a preacher."

Without warning, she lost her composure and started sobbing. "It didn't have to happen. Why did it happen? I don't know about other sisters, how they feel about each other, but I loved my sister very much. We were going to have so much fun, just like we used to. We were going to see all the shows, and go shopping, and . . ." The words melted into more tears and she sat there crying.

Hardy gave her another drink, something stronger. She swallowed it and made a face. "I'm sorry," she said. "I'm in control now. You probably want to know the same things the police did. I flew in last night. Dotty and I had been planning this visit for a long time, but we were never definite about when. So I decided to surprise her. I checked into the Regal Hotel and I called her, but she wasn't home."

"What time was that?"

"The plane landed at eight thirty. I was in the hotel by nine thirty. I was so exhausted I fell asleep. When I woke up this morning and called her again

17

a policeman answered the phone. If only I hadn't fallen asleep, I might have saved her.

"The silliest part of it all is that they asked me to account for my time last night. I checked into the hotel and fell asleep. I have no witness. I was alone. Perhaps I should have picked up some man, then I would have had a witness."

"It's just part of the routine. I'm sure they don't suspect you. Do you feel a little better now?"

"Yes," she answered softly.

Hardy got up from his desk and headed for the kitchen. "Excuse me a minute. I have to check something."

Holmes looked after Hardy for a second and then decided against following him. Instead, the dog pushed his face into Peg Robbins' lap and waited to be petted. She smiled and obliged him. Hardy returned and took in the scene. "That's the first smile I've seen on your face since you came in. How'd you like to stay for dinner? Before you answer . . . it's coq au vin, and I'm a very good cook."

She smiled again. "Why not? I have to eat, and I could use the company. I would like to call my father though."

"Is he here in New York with you?"

"No. I called him this morning. He couldn't come. But I want to tell him what I'm doing."

"Sure thing. Use the phone on the desk. I have things to do in the kitchen. If you want to wash up, the bathroom's in there."

During dinner they avoided talking about the case and anything connected with it. When she had finished her second cup of coffee, Peg sighed. "You're right. You are a good cook."

"I have many talents. How about some brandy?"

"What about the dishes?"

"No problem. Maid comes tomorrow."

They went back into the living room, and he supplied them both with brandy and cigarettes.

"O.K.," he said. "Back to business. What was the name of the officer in charge of your sister's case?"

"You won't believe this. It's Friday. Detective Friday."

"Is his first name Joe?"

"I don't know. He's black. Very nice."

"I think I'll drop in on him tomorrow. Get the lay of the land. What did your father say?"

"He's leaving everything up to me. Poor Daddy. He really liked Dot better than he did me, but he could never get through to her. And now she's dead, and he'll never be able to. She never forgave him."

"For what?"

"Daddy was born and raised a Catholic. Mother was a Protestant and the daughter of a preacher. The only way Daddy could marry Mother was to convert. Daddy's father never forgave him, and Dotty was more Grandfather's daughter than Daddy's. I remember the time Dotty went with Grandfather and spent an afternoon with some nuns. She came home bubbling. I never saw her so happy. She said when she grew up she was going to be a nun. Mother said she couldn't become a nun because she wasn't Catholic, and Daddy backed her up. He was never a very strong man. Grandfather got very angry when he heard about it. Then when Daddy decided to become a minister, that was the last straw. Grandfather never stepped foot in our house again. After that Dotty was polite to Daddy. She answered him when he said something, but they never really spoke to each other again. Not even when Mother died. Then she left home five years ago. The next time I saw her was this morning."

Peg's story bothered Hardy a great deal. He couldn't see where it would help him with the case, and it had created the wrong type of mood. No, this was definitely the wrong time to make a pass.

"Come on," he said. "I'll get you a cab."

Chapter Four

The next morning was one of those mornings. Hardy woke up with a headache and a vague recollection of dreaming about the shooting again. He used the headache as an excuse to skip his workout. Then the maid called and said she couldn't make it and he broke the yolks of his sunny side ups. As if that weren't enough, somebody's dog didn't have any manners, and Hardy slipped on the results outside his apartment and wrenched his trick knee.

Later he limped through a door marked Detectives at the police station and was pointed toward Detective Second Grade Gerald Friday. Friday nodded at a chair. "Sit down, Mr. Hardy. First things first. I've heard all the Dragnet jokes and all the Robinson Crusoe jokes. If we skip them, things will be a lot simpler. Now, what can I do for you?"

"What can you tell me about the Dorothy Robbins' case?"

"Why?" said the husky cop, running a finger over his mustache.

"I'm a private detective, and her sister hired me to investigate."

Friday laughed out loud. "You're putting me on."

"Don't laugh. I have no illusions about myself. I know catching killers is the city's job. I tried to talk her out of it, but she thinks you're on the wrong track."

"And you didn't want to pass up a fee."

"You're entitled to your opinion. Will you tell me about the case?"

"Why not? Night before last, between the hours of ten P.M. and four A.M., Dorothy Robbins, female Caucasian, aged 24, was strangled to death by a person or persons unknown. She was not raped and nothing seemed to be stolen. There was no sign of a struggle. That's it, Mr. Hardy. You'll excuse me now, huh? I've got work to do."

"Wait a minute. You said no sign of a struggle. That could mean she knew the killer."

"It could also mean she was daydreaming, or asleep, or a lot of other things."

"Was the lock forced?"

"No, but it's the slip type, a baby could open it with a credit card. Look, that building's got a bad history. About a year ago the landlord switched to self-service elevators. Since then there have been two other murders, and some nut killed a dog. And the victim herself was mugged about six months ago. Add four or five robberies to that and you have the picture."

Hardy massaged his knee and wished he were home in bed. "Who found the body?" he asked.

"The porter. He was cleaning the hall. Her door was open . . . wide open."

"Do you think he . . . ?"

"No chance. Poor scared old man. Shouldn't even be working. He's almost 80 . . . hm! . . . It's a tossup who's thinner, him or his mop."

"One final question and I'll go. How do the M.O.s of the other two killings compare with this one?"

Friday stared at him while Hardy grew very self-conscious. Hardy knew his use of the term M.O. was an attempt to sound like a "real private eye." He also knew Friday knew. Finally, Friday cleared his throat and answered his question. "First one was a 60-year-old woman. Raped and strangled. Second one was a crippled doorman. He was strangled too. His money and watch were gone. Anything else?"

"Yes. Is it all right if I enter the apartment?"

"Sure. Provided you have written permission or are accompanied by a member of the deceased's family. We have the key here. By the way, be careful. Don't let any of the Organization's bad men hurt you."

"She mentioned that to you too?"

"Isn't it exciting! Just like one of those hard-boiled murder mysteries. Everybody always getting beaten up or made love to. Gee, I wish I was a private detective."

"Very funny," said Hardy. "Very funny." As he walked to the door he could still hear Friday chuckling.

He stopped at a phone booth and called Peg and told her to pick up the key and meet him at Dorothy's apartment. Then he gorged himself at a pizza parlor and went to the apartment himself.

The doorman was out front smoking a cigarette. Hardy walked over to him.

"Excuse me."

"Yeah?"

"Are there any vacant apartments in this building?"

"Yeah. Someone just moved out day before yesterday." He cackled and lit a new cigarette from his old one. "I just made a joke. Hear about the girl who got strangled?"

Hardy nodded.

"This is where it happened."

"How terrible."

"That ain't nothin'. This is a dangerous job. Guy who worked here before me got strangled too. Don't pay you enough for this kind of job. Course he was a night man. I got the day shift. Wouldn't catch me working here at night. This ain't my regular line anyway. I was with the post office twelve years, till some rotten supervisor canned me cause he had it in for me. But I'm working on it. I won't be stuck in this creepy job forever. I got friends who are going to get me back in. Tell you what. That dead girl's apartment is going to be empty pretty soon—soon as her family gets her junk out. Make it worth my while, and I'll keep you posted.

"I don't know. It sounds too dangerous."

"Everything in New York is dangerous."

Hardy glanced up and saw Peg approaching.

"Hi, Pat. Have you been waiting long?"

"No. Just got here. What floor?"

"Five. Here's the key."

He turned back to the doorman. "Thank you."

The doorman stared at Peg, started to say something, then threw away his cigarette and said, "Wise guy."

As they rode up, Peg said nervously, "What was that all about?"

24

"I pretended I was looking for an apartment, and he didn't like being fooled. Here we are. Give me the key."

She gave it to him and fidgeted while he opened the door. As he was closing it behind them he saw a large, well-dressed, middle-aged woman leaving the adjoining apartment. He swung the door back open to get a better look. The woman stared at him for a moment and then said to the air, "Forgot something," and went back in. Hardy checked her nameplate: Amanda Delaney. He nodded his head and joined Peg in the apartment. She took off her sunglasses and asked, "Well, what do we do now?" And then, in a sudden burst, she started to cry.

"I'm sorry, Peg. I should have had more sense. You go on home. I'll finish here and call you when I get done."

"O.K. I feel so silly."

"Don't, it's only natural. Have you made any plans for the stuff here?"

"Yes, the Salvation Army is going to come by for it."

"Don't you want to keep anything?"

"Her picture, I guess. I don't want any of the clothes or furniture." She walked over to get the picture.

"Never mind, I'll get it. Tell you what. I have to look through this stuff, while I'm at it I'll collect any papers I find or anything I think you might want, and I'll take them to my place. O.K.?"

She thought for a moment and then said, "All right."

"Fine. I'll call you later."

She opened the door, looked out into the hallway, looked back at him and left. He went to work. He found an empty suitcase in the bedroom and put every

25

scrap of paper in it he could find. Phone bills, light bills, everything. Then he went to the bathroom and gathered up every pill bottle that had a prescription label on it. These joined the papers. Then he pulled all the clothing out of the closet and examined it piece by piece. Eventually he hit pay dirt. In a corner of the closet was a box. In the box was a costume straight out of the Arabian Nights: harem pants, a veil, and something more contemporary—a G-string. He examined the G-string's rhinestone surface and whistled a few bars of strip music. "If Poppa only knew," he said out loud as he turned over the pillows on the couch and the armchairs. After a quick look in the kitchen, he decided he had everything and started to leave.

His eyes fell on the dead girl's picture on the bureau. Except for her blonde hair she looked a lot like Peg. He took the picture out of the frame and found it was covering another picture . . . of a young man about 30 and fairly good looking. Across the bottom was scrawled "Love and Everything, Larry." Hardy removed that picture and found another one. This picture was one of an older, more distinguished man. There was no writing. Hardy put the three pictures in the bag and left the apartment. He thought about talking to all the people in the building and decided against it. Instead he walked over to Broadway, got a newspaper and went home.

He chased Holmes off the chaise and lay down to think. Thinking made him hungry so he went into the kitchen and finished what was left of the coq au vin. As much as he wanted to, Hardy couldn't ignore the mounting pile of dishes, so, with much grumbling to Holmes, he washed them. After checking with his answering service and finding out there were no messages, he looked through the assorted papers he had picked up in Dorothy Robbins' apartment. He found some endearing letters from someone named Larry. He assumed it was the same Larry as in the photo. There were no envelopes, therefore no address for Larry. Larry seemed to be an actor. He also kept referring to someone called Vanning, and there were questions about her "sponsor" being around.

Hardy made another assumption that Vanning and the "sponsor" and the man in the other picture were the same. He hummed another snatch of strip music while he called Steve Macker. Steve Macker was one of those handsome studs women seemed to find irresistible. He had always been, at one time or another, a stunt man, junkie, actor, crook and adventurer. Despite his moral lapses he was a very bright guy. At the moment he was trodding the straight and narrow and trying to make it as an actor in New York. Hardy had met him some months before and found him to be very useful.

"Steve Macker talking."

"Hi, Steve. Pat Hardy. You working?"

"Nope."

"I need your help."

"For how much?"

"Forty a day."

"Seventy-five," Macker countered.

"Fifty."

"A deal. Who do I kill?" asked the actor.

"No one. Tomorrow I want you to find out what you can from some tenants in a building and some local storeowners."

"What are you working on?"

"A murder."

"And you saved the exciting stuff for me. What a drag!"

27

"Stop complaining, with what I pay you this week and unemployment insurance you'll be rich. Steve, do you have one of those books that list actors, you know, with their pictures?"

"You mean a casting guide. Sure."

"Come on over and bring it with you."

"Am I on salary?"

"Not till tomorrow."

"Then why . . . ah, I'm not doing anything. Open a bottle, I'll be right over."

Hardy hung up and called Peg. He told her he didn't find too much at the apartment, but that he would call her the next day. Holmes kept bothering him, so he took the poodle out for a walk in Riverside Park. When they got back, Steve Macker was standing next to his motorcycle, waiting.

"Pat, you've got to stop taking me for granted. What's wrong with your leg?"

"Oh, hi, Steve. Sorry I'm late. Come on in. I twisted my knee. Is that the book?"

Hardy set an opened bottle of I.W. Harper in front of Steve, and while he did in the bourbon, Hardy searched through the book. Ten minutes later, he found him.

"Here he is, Larry Leeds." He showed Macker the picture. "Do you know him?"

"No, but I've seen him around. He's not bad. You want me to check him out?"

"I'll handle him myself. You don't even know what the case is all about."

"Then fill me in."

Hardy did so. When he was through, he showed Macker the pills he had taken from Dorothy's apartment.

"What do you think, expert?"

Macker put down his drink and looked at them.

"Well?" asked Hardy.

"Nothing much. These three are tranquilizers. Different types. These are sleeping pills and those capsules are dexadrine. Nothing really hard."

"Maybe. It all depends on how much she depended on them. That's a lot of pills for one person."

"Jesus, you really are square about some things, Pat. You ought to see some people's pill supply. This group here is average." He looked at the labels. "Same druggist on all of them. I'll talk to him tomorrow."

"What are the dates on those things?"

Macker looked them over. "Spring of last year."

"If she were using them at a steady rate . . . ?"

"She wouldn't have that many left. She must have been tapering off. Was there any booze in her place?"

"Son of a bitch," said Hardy. "There wasn't any. But there were all sorts of booze glasses in the kitchen. I can make two assumptions. One, somebody took the liquor before or after she died, maybe the killer, which I doubt. Or two, she felt she was drinking too much and in an effort to quit she threw it all away. Steve, check the super about her garbage . . . if she threw away a lot of bottles recently."

"I'm way ahead of you. Anything else?"

"Take these bills with you and check out her butcher and laundry, and don't forget the old man who found her, the porter, and . . . ah, you know the rest."

"Got you. How about an advance?"

Hardy gave him twenty dollars. "Don't spend it all in one place. Leave the casting guide with me, and call me tomorrow when you're finished."

Macker had another drink, left his empty glass on the floor and went.

29

Hardy wandered around the apartment for a minute. He started a tub going and got food out for Holmes, who was licking Macker's empty glass.

He looked at Larry Leeds' picture in the book and checked for Dorothy Robbins. She was there. According to the book, both of them had been on the road in the same play the summer before. He went into the kitchen and got everything ready for a dinner of chile con carne. As he walked to the door, he started undressing. He set the police lock and went into the bathroom for his bath. Hardy sat in the tub soaking and massaging his knee, thinking about the case for a moment and then pushing it out of his mind. Instead he thought about the chile, the new science fiction book he had bought and all the great shows that were on television that night.

Chapter Five

It was a better day. His knee was fine, and he hadn't dreamed. Hardy felt so good he even enjoyed his morning workout.

The maid arrived just as he finished breakfast.

"Morning, Mr. Hardy. Sorry about yesterday."

"Morning, Laura. Don't worry about it. If the phone rings, let the service pick up. I'll be right back. Come on, Holmes, let's go."

While Holmes enriched the soil in Riverside Park, Hardy tried to plot out his day. No use. He couldn't concentrate. He opened the book he just happened to have with him and started reading. When he finished the book, it was afternoon and he was very hungry. He went back to the apartment and checked his answering service. No messages. He was hungry, but he was too lazy to cook. There was a great Chinese restaurant on 127th Street, and since Larry Leeds lived on West 107th Street, it would be on the way. He talked himself into it.

Hardy parked his VW on Broadway under the el next to the No Parking sign and went into the restaurant.

"Hello, Mr. Hardy. Good to see you again."

"Hello, Henry. How about some beef and oyster sauce . . . and some shrimp and black bean sauce . . . and I'll start off with egg roll."

He finished eating and phoned his service. Steve Macker had called and left word that he would meet him at six at Hardy's apartment. Peg Robbins had called and would call again. Hardy paid his check and headed out.

"Great meal, Henry, I'll be back in an hour."

Henry grinned and said nothing. Hardy had been using that same corny remark for over a year now.

As he was opening the car door, Hardy was startled by a loud report that sounded like a gun shot. He turned around. Three black kids who were playing with firecrackers looked at him and laughed. The oldest one pointed at Hardy and said, "White man's scared. White man's scared." He kept saying it as Hardy drove away. Hardy managed to rationalize the incident away but not before it started him thinking about the idiocy of messing around with murder. He resolved to tell Peg he was dropping the case. He stopped for a red light and saw that he was at 108th Street. As long as he was here he would see Larry Leeds.

The downstairs door was unlocked so Hardy went right up. He knocked at apartment 3F.

"Just a minute," someone said.

After a little more than that minute had gone by, the door was opened. "Hello. What can I do for you?"

Hardy had his card case ready. He flashed it quickly

32

and said, "I'm Hardy. Detective. I'd like to talk to you about the murder of Dorothy Robbins."

"Wait a minute. I . . ."

"You know of course by law you don't have to talk to me. You want to call your lawyer—go ahead."

"I know all about that stuff. I played a cop on a TV show once. What do you want to know?"

"Anything you can tell me about Dorothy Robbins."

"That's a long story."

"Tell it."

"I met her last summer. We were in a show together. You want a beer?"

"No."

"Well, I'm going to have one." He went into the kitchen.

Harry lit a cigarette. "Stop stalling."

Leeds came back out with his beer. "Who's stalling? We had a thing. It lasted during the run of the show, and then it was over. Happens all the time."

"Who called it off?"

"Nobody. It just ended."

Then why did you keep writing to her afterward?"

"We were still friends."

Hardy made a face.

"All right," said Leeds. "I still dug her. She said she couldn't afford to have me around. Some john in New York was keeping her, and while it was great fun on the road, she had to be practical in New York."

Hardy smiled. "Vanning, huh?"

"How'd you know?"

"You ever meet him?"

"Once. We were playing Detroit. He surprised her with a visit. He's a businessman of some sort . . .

33

flies all over the country. Anyway, he showed up and walked into her dressing room while I happened to be there. Luckily we weren't touching or anything like that. We were introduced, and he invited me to join them for a drink. I thought it would be cute to accept. Dot gave me hell later for that little trick. You know what he told her? He said he thought I was a fag. Ironic, wasn't it? I was balling the chick he was paying the bills for, and he thought I was a fag. His horns must have been hurting him. Anyway, he stayed around for a couple of days. I was really miserable.

"I remember the day he was supposed to leave he went to the airport and left his airline credit card in her room. She called me and told me he had gone. There was no matinee that day, and I was looking forward to spending the rest of the day with her. Then she called me back and told me he was coming back because of the card and there wouldn't be another plane till after six. That did it. I went out and got drunk. Luckily I ended up in the bar next to the theater. Probably wasn't luck at all. I guess I wanted her to find me there. She did. She sobered me up and got me on stage too. I know it's a cliché line, but I can't believe she's gone. When I read about it, nothing happened to me. I mean inside. I didn't even cry, and I loved her . . . I still love her. You know what I did? I hit myself in the face to make myself cry. I couldn't. Hey, you're really getting your money's worth. That's what makes me a good actor, I suppose. I'll show my emotions to anyone. Now that you've peeked at my insides, why don't you go away?"

"This is no fun for me, Mr. Leeds. Just a couple of

34

more questions. What's Vanning's full name and where does he live?"

"His first name is Joe or Jim or something like that. I think she said he lived on West End Avenue somewhere in the nineties. I don't really know."

"How would you describe him?"

"Sandy hair, a little gray. Over six feet. He's around 40 . . . 45. Good physique, but starting to get a pot, and the face is fleshy too. Too much booze I guess. Good looking. Yeah, he's good looking. I think he has a wife. Sophisticated red neck. He went to the right schools, but he shines in loud brassy bars."

Hardy was getting uncomfortable. He didn't like Leeds. The actor wasn't talking to him, he was playing a part from some corny movie and enjoying it.

"Mr. Leeds, would you happen to have a program of the play you two were in?"

"Sure." Leeds put down his beer and got a manila envelope from the bedroom. He scrounged through it till he found the program. "Here it is. Just your luck, I have two." He handed the program to Hardy and went back to his beer.

"Thank you. One more thing, Mr. Leeds. Do you know where Miss Robbins and Vanning met or how they met?"

"I don't know."

"Did you know she had been a stripper?"

"Yeah, I knew. That's why she went out on the road with our show. She wanted to go legit. Funny joke. She didn't like stripping. Actually the stripping wasn't so bad, it was the places she did it in and the creeps she met there."

"Did she meet Vanning in one of those places?"

"I asked her that once. She told me to mind my own business."

"One more thing. Did . . . ?"

"Why do you always say one more thing and then keep talking?"

"Last question. I promise. Did she use pills or drink a lot?"

"Yeah. She managed to get the pills under control, but she always needed the bottle. Hell, I don't like liquor much. But when I couldn't get her to stop, I started just to keep her company. That time she found me in the bar and dried me out, she was very happy. I finally did the normal thing as far as she was concerned. Look, I loved Dotty, but she was a bottle baby. I guess the girl she used to be was trying to run away from the girl she had become. She was a very unhappy girl." Leeds looked at him strangely. "Let me see that I.D. again. I bet you're not a cop. You don't look like a cop. Show me your badge."

Hardy ignored him. "Where were you the night she was killed?"

"I get it. You must be a private detective. Who're you working for? . . . Who cares? For your information I went to a movie that night—alone."

"Did you kill her?"

"No! Now get out of here before I call the real cops."

Hardy took out one of his cards and dropped it on the table. "Just in case."

"Get out."

It was after six when Hardy pulled up in front of his apartment. Macker was waiting for him.

"What did you find out, Steve?"

"Nothing much, and it cost you an extra ten dollars."

"What for?"

"Candy bars. That's what I used to see people.

Gave away samples. Most of them claimed they didn't even know the girl."

"What about those who did?"

"Just to say hello to. It was a bad day for it, Pat. Every place I went I was stepping on the heels of a cop. He was after the same information I was."

"That figured."

"He mooched five of the candy bars."

"That also figures. What about across the hall, 5B, Mrs. Delaney?"

Macker checked his notebook. "She didn't even want the candy. Wouldn't open the door. Why?"

"No special reason. What else do you have, Steve?"

"Super said no large amount of booze bottles in garbage. Grocer, druggist, butcher all say she was O.K., pleasant person and all that. But she was just another customer."

"How'd she pay?"

"Cash. All the time. Never ran up a bill. You're all out of bourbon."

"You finished it yesterday. Drink something else."

Macker looked over the liquor supply while Hardy got out the folder on the Robbins' case. "I know," said Macker, "I'll have a martini. The porter told me the same story he told the cops. You find out anything?"

Hardy pulled out Vanning's picture. "I'm pretty sure this guy's name is Jim or Joe Vanning and that he was paying a lot of the bills for Dorothy Robbins."

"Goddamn it, Pat. Your vermouth is bad. Look at it, it's brown. How long have you had it?"

"I don't know. I don't drink martinis. What's wrong with straight gin?"

"Nothing." Macker poured himself a drink and threw a ball for Holmes to chase. "What next?"

Hardy didn't answer, went into the kitchen, looked in the refrigerator, grabbed a banana and returned to the office. Macker and Holmes were playing tug of war with the ball. Hardy crossed to his desk and dialed the phone. "Regal Hotel."

"Peg Robbins, please. Holmes, shut up. Keep it down, will you, Steve."

"Hello."

"Hello, Peg? Pat Hardy. Could I see you tonight? Something I . . ."

"I'm sorry, Pat. I'll be busy with Mr. Wilson tonight. He's the funeral director."

"What about tomorrow then? I'll buy you lunch."

"The funeral is tomorrow."

"Oh. Well then . . . uh, I'll buy you dinner then."

"That will be fine."

"I'll pick you up about seven. So long."

He hung up the phone and took out his checkbook. "Thanks for your help, Steve. Fifty plus ten minus twenty equals forty dollars, right?"

"Right. You going to be needing me any more?"

"I don't think so. I think I'll drop it and tell my client to go home. I was going to tell her now, but . . ."

"But what?"

"She was talking to the funeral director. Funeral's tomorrow."

"Shouldn't you be there?"

"Yeah, if I were staying on the case. I've got no business messing around with murder cases. You doing anything tonight?"

"Nope."

"Come on. I'll buy you dinner and then we'll do a little serious drinking."

"Best offer I've had all day."

38

After a meal of ziti a la Siciliana and a bottle of chianti, Hardy and Macker grabbed a cab and headed downtown. They made the rounds of a few bars, then Macker led them to a strip joint. Hardy laughed.

"Steve, you're too much. I told you I was dropping the case. What's the idea of coming here?"

"Screw you and your case. I just want to see a little flesh, that's all."

"I believe you. But I'm sitting at the bar. I'm not going to buy some B-girl cold tea for three bucks a shot."

They entered as the band was introducing a new stripper.

"How's that for timing?" said Macker, and he ordered two drinks. Hardy pretended indifference and looked around the room. "If I want to look at naked women, I want them in my bedroom where I can do something about it."

The girl came out. She was young and very pretty. She was dressed in a *Swan Lake*-type ballet costume and had a stuffed swan as a prop. She placed the swan in the middle of the stage and as the band played their rendition of *Swan Lake*, the girl did a ballet strip.

Hardy grew interested. Also, he grew aroused. The girl's first turn was over. Her headpiece and extraneous scarves were gone. She stood on her toes over the swan and danced around it. The music increased its tempo and she moved faster and faster, offering herself to the swan and forgetting all pretense of ballet. Her red hair, which had been done up in a bun, was now down, flowing wildly, and she had gotten rid of more clothing so that now she was down to G-string and net bra.

As the lights switched to a purple hue, Hardy

39

drained his drink and lit a cigarette. The girl was on the floor now, caressing the swan and kissing it and then rubbing its beak over her breasts and loins. She placed it back on the stage and knelt before it with her back to the audience. She placed the bird between her legs and leaned her body back so that her hair touched the floor. Her eyes were closed as if in ecstasy, her arms were outstretched to some unseen lover. As the music grew more frantic, so did she, vibrating to the music and arching her body more and more till her face and her breasts were now pointing toward the audience, more erotic because of her upside-down position. The music reached its climax and so, it seemed, did she. The lights changed to a brilliant red as she ripped off the net bra and screamed. Blackout. Then silence. The lights came back up and she was standing centerstage, holding the swan to her bosom and bowing. Suddenly, as if from a mechanical source, the applause and whistles started.

Macker ordered another round and turned to Hardy. "Some stuff, huh? And you didn't want to come in."

Hardy sipped his drink and nodded. He lit a cigarette and took a few drags. "A very superior performance, I must say."

"Would I steer you wrong?" Macker asked.

"Well," Hardy said, "now that I'm all nervous and bothered, what do we do?"

"We could grab a couple of these ladies who are mingling among us and take them away from all this."

"Are you crazy? First we'll have to buy a lot of phony booze, and then they'll make a date that they'll never keep, and we'll end up with each other. No thanks. I'm going to make a few phone calls, and if nobody's home, I'm going home to take a cold shower."

"Relax, Pat. Trust your old buddy."

Macker disappeared into the mob while Hardy looked around. The management called it a night-club but it was just a bar with a stage. There were girls leaning against the bar. When her turn came, each one would do a strip act. When they weren't stripping they were out on the floor mixing and hustling drinks. One caught his eye and headed over to where he was. "Hi. Buy a girl a drink?"

"No."

"Aw, come on. Be a sport."

"Go away, girlie. Find yourself a live one."

"Creep." With that she went looking for a live one. There seemed to be quite a few too. Hotshots from out of town who would pay twenty dollars for bad sauterne mixed with seltzer, and another ten dollars for a cheap job under the table and then maybe as much as fifty dollars for the promise of a meeting that would never take place. As Hardy took this all in, he spotted two men who didn't seem to fit. They didn't look like the usual suckers who came to places like this. They also didn't look like the general order of mugs who were a part of the establishment. The older one looked like an ad for distinguished executive of the year. His companion was about 35 and good looking in a slimy sort of way. Both were very well tailored and looked like money. Hardy wasn't sure, but he thought he knew the younger man. While he was trying to figure out from where, Macker came back with two girls.

"Well, Pat, what did I tell you? This is Milly and Ginger. Ginger is mine."

"You can have them both."

41

Milly poked Hardy with her breasts. "Don't be mean, sweetie."

"Come on," Macker whispered. "I've got an angle. Hey, girls, do you have a private dressing room?"

Milly started rubbing Hardy's knee and purred in his ear. "Ginger has her own dressing room, she's featured. We could all go there and drink and things."

Macker grabbed Hardy's arm. "I heard that. Great. Let's go."

Hardy shook him off. "Steve, this feels like trouble."

Macker put his hand on Ginger's ass. "It feels good to me. Come on, Pat. Relax and have some fun."

"Before we have fun, who are those two guys?" Hardy nodded at the two men he had spotted before.

Macker glanced at them. "The one with the gray hair is Louis White. Runs a real estate firm. Very important, in Big Business, and in other places."

"What does that mean?"

"You figure it out. The other one is always with him. Sort of a friend and bodyguard, Ben Pelligrin. I don't know what he ever did, but I bet he was mean about it. Now, let's forget that stuff and get it on."

"Yeah," said Milly. "Let's get it on."

Ginger took out a cigarette and lit it from the one in Macker's hand. "We're going back there now. Wait five minutes and then follow us." Milly detached herself from Hardy and followed Ginger out. Macker watched them as they went. "That's nice stuff, Pat."

"I don't know about that. Mine has rough elbows."

Macker laughed so hard he started choking. After he controlled his coughing, he had a beer to wash it down. "Pat, you're too much. You're chicken, that's what. Rough elbows!"

"Well she did, sort of like calluses . . . Wait a minute, I bet they all have it, occupational hazard."

"What are you talking about?"

"Use your head. It's obvious. They get it from leaning on the bar with their elbows."

"Marvelous," the actor said. "I couldn't have lived without that information. Now let's go."

"Wait a minute. How'd you get them to agree to this?"

"I promised Ginger a hundred dollars. She's greedy."

"I have enough faith in you to realize you won't pay it," said Hardy. "But what about Milly?"

"She's just horny. She'll go anywhere with anyone."

"Thanks a lot."

"You're welcome," said Macker and finished his drink. He looked around and strolled back toward the dressing rooms. Hardy thought about being home, and then much against his better judgment, he followed Macker. A rough type with a flat nose stopped Hardy. "Where do you think you're going?"

"To the men's room."

"Well, it ain't back here."

Hardy was ready to forget about it when someone called the rough type. "Hey, George, come here a minute." George went to wherever "here" was, leaving Hardy a clear path. He went down the empty hall, trying to figure out his next move. A door opened, and Macker poked his head out. "Pat, inside." Hardy examined the small cubicle and said, "What now?"

Milly giggled.

"Let's have a drink," said Macker.

Ginger sat down at the dressing table and checked her makeup. "You bring anything with you?"

"No," said Steve. "But I bet you have some."

"Sure she does," said Milly. "Her body cologne."

Hardy sat down. "Her what?"

Ginger tried to quiet her, but Milly went blithely on. "We're not supposed to have booze back here so Ginger hides it in this bottle and calls it body cologne."

Macker grabbed the cologne bottle and sniffed it, then he drank. "Scotch. I'm a bourbon man myself, but this will do. Here, Pat, drink up."

They passed the bottle around a few times, and Milly and the two men were quite happy. Ginger wasn't amused. She kept taking Macker aside and whispering to him. "Relax, honey," he said. "I'll take care of you."

Milly was all over Hardy and making him very nervous. "Steve."

"Yeah, Pat."

"This isn't going to work out. Too crowded here."

Macker went over to the window which led out to the alley. "You're right, Pat, it is too crowded. I have an idea. You girls have to go on any more tonight?"

"No," said Milly, as she had another drink.

"Good," said Macker. "Ginger and I will go to her place, and you and Milly can do what you want to."

"Wait a minute," said Ginger. "We're supposed to stay and mix."

Macker opened the window. "Don't worry about it. Come on, relax and enjoy life. Besides . . ." He whispered the rest in Ginger's ear, and her greed got the better of her.

"All right," she said. "But if we're going, let's go fast."

"That's more like it," said Macker, as he finished the contents of the cologne bottle. "Pat, you go out first and then help Milly."

Hardy was quite drunk. So was everybody else in the room. He climbed out the window, and as he helped Milly out, she nearly fell. She squealed in mock horror. Hardy yelled, "Alley Oop," and Macker, who was enjoying himself tremendously, started laughing.

"Sh," said Ginger. "They'll hear us."

"So what!" said Macker. "We're leaving."

He was handing her out the window to Hardy when somebody knocked at the door.

"What the hell is going on in there?" Without waiting for an answer, the owner of the voice shoved the door open. This was very impressive since the door had been locked.

"What do you think you're doing?" It was George, the rough type from the hall. He charged at Macker and knocked him to the floor. By this time Hardy and the girls were outside looking in.

"Oh," said Milly. "That's George, the bouncer. He'll kill him."

George kicked Macker in the ribs. Ginger lit a cigarette, and Milly screamed. She poked Hardy. "Why don't you go in and help him?" Hardy stood there and swallowed the sour spit that had collected in his mouth. George aimed a kick at Macker's head. Macker grabbed the foot and pushed. As George bounced off the wall, Macker jumped up and poked some fingers in George's throat. George gagged and vomited and slumped to the floor. Macker looked for a second to make sure George wasn't getting up. He closed the door and went out the window. "Some fun, hey, Pat? Come on, Ginger, we're wasting time. See you, Pat."

Macker and Ginger grabbed a passing cab and were gone. There were no other cabs available so Hardy took Milly's arm and started walking. After a while he realized he had to use a men's room, and fast.

"Milly, do you live far from here?"

"49th Street. Look, there's a cab."

As the cab took them uptown Hardy thought about his fear. He shook it off with the rationalization that Macker had gotten out of the situation all right.

"We're here, honey."

He paid the driver and they got out. Hardy was a mess. He was drunk; he was frightened. He wanted to make love, and he wanted to urinate. Once more he wished he had stayed home. Inside the hallway Milly pressed herself against him. He wasn't sure, but he thought her embrace was a maneuver so she could ring one of the bells. She pulled away and caressed his face.

"What are we waiting down here for? Let's go upstairs."

The apartment was one of those nondescript places that are so common in midtown Manhattan, complete with the management's cheap Grand Rapids furniture and the 42nd Street renditions of Modigliani and Keane. She grabbed him and kissed him again. She bit his tongue and opened his jacket. He pushed her away. "First things first. Where's the john?"

"In there."

He went into the bathroom and relieved himself. While he was luxuriating in the pleasure of a voided bladder, he realized that he hadn't had to lift the toilet seat. He lit a cigarette and thought about it.

Why would a woman leave the seat up? No reason. The only reason the seat would be up would be so a man could use it. That could mean she had a lot of men coming in and out. It could also mean there was a man here now, waiting for his chance. His fear returned. With this in mind he went out into the other room. Milly was standing there. Stark naked. Hardy forgot his fear and went over to her. He looked at her breasts glistening with perspiration. She licked her lips and turned toward the bedroom. He watched her ass as it walked away from him and he followed it into the bedroom. She was on the bed.

As he loosened his tie the private detective heard a noise behind him. He turned in time to see the blackjack coming at his head. His mind ran away and his reflexes took over. He grabbed the hand holding the blackjack and pulled it in the direction of the swing. As his attacker went by, Hardy chopped him in the neck and then in the kidneys. Down he went. Hardy picked him up to finish him off.

Milly screamed. "Stop, you'll kill him."

Hardy stopped, looked at the man in his hands and dropped him. He was back to normal now, and he started shaking. Milly was still on the bed. The new violence had excited her. "You're too much, lover. I didn't think you had it in you."

"Who is that?"

"That's Charlie. Forget about him and come here. I need a man like you."

"What about him?"

"Throw him in the closet or something."

Hardy dragged Charlie to the closet. He locked the door and stood there, breathing heavily. Milly

47

got out of the bed and led Hardy back to it. She took off his clothes and caressed him as she did. Her caresses brought him back to the matter at hand, and all in all, it was quite a night.

Chapter Six

Hardy opened his eyes. It was morning and he was thirsty. He looked around, realized where he was, and went to the bathroom. The water he drank seemed to help, but he was still groggy so he got into the shower and turned on the cold water. It worked. He grabbed the largest towel he could find and wrapped it around himself and went into the kitchen. All he found in the refrigerator was a bottle of ketchup and an orange. He ate the orange.

He went into the bedroom to get his clothes. Milly was just opening her eyes. She took a cigarette from the night table and lit up. "Don't go, sweetie. Come back to bed."

Hardy saw the mess of mascara and lipstick that was her face and looked out the window. "No thanks, Milly. I appreciate the offer, but I've got things to do."

"O.K. But don't be a stranger. Come back anytime."

"What about Charlie?"

"Oh, my God! I forgot about him. I better let him out."

"Wait till I leave if you don't mind. Is he a good friend?"

"No, he's my husband."

As Hardy finished getting dressed, he thought about Dorothy Robbins. As long as he was here he would take advantage of it. "Milly? Did you ever know a stripper called Dorothy Robbins?"

"Honey, I like you a lot. But ask me no questions, I'll tell you no lies."

"Milly, I'll make a deal with you. I won't tell the cops that you and your husband are playing games, and you answer my question."

"All right. I never knew her. She used to do an act about a year ago. She called herself Scheherazade. Wore a harem costume. You know, those baggy pants and a veil."

"What else, Milly?"

"Don't tell her I told you, but Ruby knew her."

"Who's Ruby?"

"Ruby Red. You saw her last night. The one with the swan."

Hardy knotted his tie and ran a comb through his hair. "Thanks, Milly. Regards to Charlie."

When he got home he brushed his teeth, shaved and took another shower. He made up a batch of buckwheat cakes and fried lots of bacon and watched a movie on television while he had breakfast. He fed Holmes, took *My Life and Loves* from the bookshelf, went to bed and read himself to sleep.

By eleven thirty Holmes grew bored with lying at his master's feet and started playing a game called "jump on and off the bed."

"I'm up. You win. I'm up."

Hardy got dressed and took Holmes out for a run to the park. When they got back he called information and checked on J. Vanning. Not listed. Then he called information again for the number of Wilson's Funeral Home. As he waited for information to find it for him, he realized that he had put himself back on the case. "Thank you, operator."

He dialed the number the operator had given him.

"Wilson's Funeral Home. Lester Wilson speaking."

"Mr. Wilson, my name is Patrick Hardy, and I work for Peg Robbins."

"Oh, yes. The sister of the late Dorothy Robbins. It's sad when they go so young."

"Yes, it is. Could I please talk to the person who prepared the body for burial?"

"I am that person. We are not a large concern, Mr. Hardy. I give very personal service."

"Mr. Wilson, I know this may sound strange, but did you notice whether or not the deceased has calluses on her elbows?"

"I beg your pardon."

"I know it's a strange question, but . . ."

"I wish I could help you, Mr. Hardy, but I just don't recall. I wish I could help you."

"Thank you very much, Mr. Wilson. I wish you could help me too. Good-bye."

The phone rang as soon as he hung it up. "Hello."

"Hi, Pat. Steve. How are you feeling today?"

"Oh, hello, Steve. I'm fine. How are you?"

"Layed. Relayed and parlayed."

"Sounds like fun," he chuckled. "You didn't pay her, did you?"

"Are you kidding? She should have paid me. How was yours?"

"O.K. Except she pulled a con on me. Lucky for

me I was faster than her partner was . . . Everything turned out fine."

"I'm glad to hear it. I felt a little responsible for you."

"I bet," said Hardy. "You want to do some work for me today?"

"You got another case?"

"No. Same one. I changed my mind."

"I'm beat; besides, I have to go see about a commercial this afternoon. Hey, put my helmet where it won't get lost."

"O.K. You need it?"

"No, I have a spare."

"Call me tomorrow."

"Right."

Hardy had planned to loaf the rest of the day, but with Macker unavailable . . . ? He got old clothes that he kept for such purposes out of the closet and put them on.

It really wasn't necessary, but he combed his hair in a different manner and added prop glasses to complete the effect. Now he looked the way he thought a delivery boy might look.

After admiring himself in the mirror he got a plain envelope from his desk, stuffed it with a blank piece of paper and addressed it to Mr. J. Vanning. As an afterthought he marked it "By Hand."

He drove up the Drive to 100th Street and parked between the Drive and West End Avenue. Then he tried to deliver his letter. He went down West End to 90th and up West End back to 100th. No luck. Hardy got back into his car and drove over to Broadway to a delicatessen he knew. He had a corned-beef sandwich and potato salad and cream soda and felt much better. Then he drove to 90th and West

End and started again. At 88th Street he got lucky.
"Hey, who do you want?"

Hardy smiled at the doorman and stuttered.
"L-l-letter for M-mister V-v-vanning." He had read
somewhere that people don't like to look directly at
people who stutter. The doorman looked at the
envelope and shook his head.

"Joseph Vanning hasn't lived here for over six
months. Stupid people. Wait a minute. I'll look in
my book and get his new address for you." The
doorman went to a table and took a notebook out
of a drawer. He muttered as he looked through it.
"Here it is."

He grabbed the envelope from Hardy's hand.

"I'll write it down for you so you don't forget."
Hardy grinned as he watched the doorman write
down an address in the East Fifties. He was very
pleased that his ploy had worked.

The doorman shoved the envelope back at him.

"Here, kid. Don't get lost."

He whistled as he drove downtown. Tomorrow he
would see Vanning. But now he was going to relax.

He watched television till six, fed Holmes and
then got dressed for dinner.

He decided against the car and caught the bus to
the Regal Hotel.

When Peg came to the door she had a drink in her
hand all ready for him. "Hi! Hey, you look neat.
Better hurry, I'm two drinks up on you."

Hardy did a take on her new appearance. She had
had long hair when he first met her. Now it was
short.

"Hi. What did you do to your hair?"

"I was bored."

"Looks nice. You have any preference about dinner?"

"Let's eat in tonight. It's so nice and . . . safe here. The food's not bad. O.K.?"

"O.K."

He reached into his pocket for a letter he had prepared for her. "Look this over while I call room service for a waiter."

"What is it?"

"A letter to the post office requesting that your sister's mail be forwarded to me. I doubt if it will do any good, but who knows, I might get lucky." He handed her a pen and picked up the phone. "Room service, please. Anything wrong?" he asked her. She fingered the letter for a moment and then signed it.

"Good," he said as he put it away. "That takes care of business. The rest is pleasure." He spoke to the phone again. "Send a waiter to 503, please."

Dinner was over and the dishes had been cleared. Peg smiled at him over another drink. "See, I told you the food was good. So's the liquor. Drink up, Pat. Drink up . . . for tomorrow we die. Drink to Dottie. Good-bye, Dottie. You were a great girl. But it's good-bye forever now. And you're never never ever coming back. You know, nobody but me went to her funeral. Poor Dorothy, you thought you had so many friends, and nobody even came to your funeral."

"Cut it out, Peg. You'll only make yourself sick. I'd ease off the sauce too if I were you."

"You would, would you? Let me tell you something, mister . . . ah, never mind. If you only knew, if you only knew."

"Come on, Peg. You're not used to that stuff. You don't realize the price you're going to have to pay in the morning."

54

"Couple of Bufferin and I'll be fine. Don't be a party poop, Pat. Hey, try saying that five times fast. Don't be a . . . You're not going to let them get away with it, are you? Those rats killed. . . . that damn Organization. You've got to get them, Pat. Promise me that you'll get them."

"I promise."

"Pat? Do you think I'm pretty?"

"Yes, I do."

"I have a great figure. Want to see?" She got up and walked over to him. She stared at him coquettishly and started singing. "A pretty girl is like a melody . . ." As she sang she tried to open the top button on her dress. "Come on, Pat. Don't just sit there. Help a lady out. Open the damn button for me."

"Sit down, Peg, and I'll order up some coffee."

"I don't want any goddamn coffee. What's the matter, aren't I good enough for you? Don't I excite you?"

"As a matter of fact, you do. Very much."

"What's the matter? Conscience? Won't take advantage of the poor girl because she's had too much to drink? What are you, a Boy Scout?"

"Nope, I just don't want you going to sleep on me in the middle. I'll take a rain check though. Good night, Peg."

"Why you . . . You know what you are? You're a . . ."

He never did find out what he was. Without any warning, Peg sat down hard on the couch and sprawled like a bag of potatoes. She closed her eyes and was out. Hardy shook his head and lit a cigarette.

As he was putting out the cigarette, she opened her eyes and tried focus on him. "Carry me to bed. . . ." He did just that, he took her into the bedroom, and she snuggled closer in his arms. She had a great figure and, even though she was slobbering drunk, Hardy found her exciting. He was sorry she had had so much to drink.

Hardy placed the girl on the bed and covered her and headed for the door. Halfway there he changed his mind and came back and looked at her lovely inert body. He placed a hand on her breast and thought about next time. After this bit of self-indulgence, he left her room and went home.

Chapter Seven

Hardy never did get to see Vanning the next day. During the night he had been awakened by the phone ringing, but by the time he answered it, the caller had hung up. His answering service told him it had been Larry Leeds. Hardy grunted a "thank you" and went back to sleep.

In the morning he was finishing his breakfast of corned beef hash when he remembered the phone call and checked his service to verify his memory. The girl told him the call had been made at three thirty. Hardy called Leeds but got no answer, so he had another cup of coffee and thought about Peg.

He was still thinking about Peg when he got into his car. The Regal Hotel wasn't on the way to Vanning's place, but he drove there anyway.

The desk clerk tried to ring Peg's room, but her phone seemed to be off the hook. Hardy rushed up to her room, not knowing what to expect but fearing the worst. There was no basis for his fear, but he had been jumpy ever since he started this case. He barged into her room. There she was, on the floor, sound asleep. Hardy laughed at himself while he put her back into bed and put the phone back on the receiver. The desk clerk rang and the private detective told him everything was all right. After he hung up, Hardy stood there and admired Peg's body. She must have gotten up during the night and changed into a nightgown. It was very sheer. He went into the bathroom and dampened a washcloth with warm water. He took the washcloth into the bedroom and placed it gently on Peg's face. "Come on, Sleeping Beauty, time to get up."

"Go away."

She was still asleep and kept moving her head away as Hardy washed her face with the cloth. "Come on, Peg. Get up."

"I don't want to. Hold me. Hold me close." Her eyes snapped open, and she gasped. "Don't . . . don't . . ." Then she realized where she was and who Hardy was. "Oh, Pat . . . it's you."

"That must have been some nightmare. I told you too much sauce is no good for you."

"I should have listened to you. What a horrible nightmare!" Peg stared vacantly into space and then turned to Hardy and smiled. "What are you doing here? I thought after last night I'd never see you again."

"I'm a glutton for punishment. Besides, you're a client."

"Is that why you came back?"

"No. I was on my way to see a man, and I remembered that I never brought you up to date on the case."

"That can wait another ten minutes while I take

a shower. Why don't you order us some coffee? Oh, my head! I need it. I know, you told me so."

Hardy ordered coffee and tried Larry Leeds again. Still no answer.

The coffee arrived, and Hardy poured himself a cup and lit a cigarette. Peg came out of the shower and stole them both from him. As she drank and smoked, she sighed. "There, now I feel a little more human. Hello, Pat. You're nice to look at in the morning."

"You're nice to look at all the time. Especially when you're wet and your robe is sticking to you."

She looked down at her breasts which were clearly outlined against the wet material of her robe. "If you can't stand the heat, stay out of the kitchen." She flashed a mischievous smile at him and went into the bedroom. She called back to him, "Bring me up to date while I get dressed."

"Did your sister ever mention a Larry Leeds or Joseph Vanning? Hey, did you hear me?"

"I heard you. I was thinking. No, I don't think so. Who are they?"

"Two guys she used to see," Hardy shouted to her. "I've met Leeds. Nothing. I plan on seeing Vanning today. Did your sister drink much?"

"I don't know. Why?"

"From the evidence in the apartment she kept liquor in the place, but there wasn't any when I checked."

Peg came back into the living room. "That's strange. Maybe somebody in the building took it. You know, the handyman or someone."

"Could be. Did you know your sister was a strip-per?"

"What! That's ridiculous! You couldn't be more

59

wrong. When we were kids she wouldn't even get undressed in front of me."

Hardy finished his coffee. "Well, somewhere along the way she changed. Now you know as much as I do. You want me to keep at it?"

"Yes. I know I sound like a silly broken record, but you're wasting your time with Vanning and . . . the other fellow."

"Leeds."

"You're wasting your time there. The Organization did it. Can't you see, if you're right about her being a stripper, it fits in?"

"How do you know Vanning and Leeds aren't a part of the Organization?"

"You're right, I don't." She sipped some coffee. "I must owe you some money."

"A few dollars."

"Why don't I give you some on account."

Hardy grinned. "I won't object."

She went back into the bedroom and came out with a wad of money.

"Here," she said, as she peeled off the bills. "Five hundred. That ought to keep us up to date."

"Not counting expenses. We'll settle that when— and if—we ever figure this thing out. You always keep a lot of money around?"

"I just cashed a check. I don't like paying for things by check. Seems like so much monopoly money."

"Be careful. By now you should know what kind of a town this is."

"You're just a worrywart." As she came over to give him the money, she leaned over and kissed him, like a sister. Hardy didn't take it that way.

He pulled her to him and made the kiss long and hard. She pulled away. "Hey, steady. Not now,

60

thank you. I've got a rotten hangover . . . which you predicted, and you've got work to do. You're on my time, remember?"

"Yes, boss. That's another rain check you owe me."

"Oh. Where are you going now? To see Vanning?"

"No." He got up and went to the door. "First I'm going home to take a cold shower."

As a matter of fact he did go home, but not to take a shower. Pat Hardy believed in the old adage "Never carry more money with you than you can afford to lose." And he could never afford to lose five hundred dollars. He placed the money in the safe behind the George Grosz drawing and called Larry Leeds again. When he got no answer, he looked up Leeds in the casting guide and got the number of his answering service and called them. They said they had no idea where he was, in fact, they were trying to reach him themselves. Hardy considered the problem and decided he should go to Leeds' apartment.

As he drove uptown he bugged himself for not calling Leeds back when the actor had phoned during the night. Again, Hardy had the feeling that something terrible had happened. He had been wrong the last time, but he still had the feeling.

This time he was right. Leeds' door was unlocked. When Hardy opened it he saw Leeds lying on the floor with a pair of scissors in his back. The place looked as if it had been struck by a tornado. Papers and books were all over the floor. Hardy took a closer look at the body and felt sick. When he recovered he made a quick search of his own and came up empty. Then he called Detective Gerald Friday.

"Friday speaking."

"This is Pat Hardy."

61

"Who? . . . Oh, yeah. The private detective. What can I do for you?"

"It's what I can do for you. I want to report another murder."

"Hardy, if you're making jokes, I'll crown you."

"No joke. Fellow by the name of Larry Leeds was stabbed to death in his apartment. It might interest you to know he was a friend of Dorothy Robbins."

"O.K. Where is it?"

"107th Street and Broadway. It's the corner."

"Hardy, why are you breaking my chops? That's not even in my precinct."

"But I thought . . ."

"Never mind what you thought. You've been reading too many books where one police station handles all the crimes. Now call 911. Better still, call the proper precinct and be quick about it."

Hardy jerked his head away as Friday slammed the phone down. He entertained a few choice thoughts about Friday, then called information to get the number of the precinct. After he spoke to the precinct he sat down to wait and looked at Leeds as he waited. The dead man was wearing only shorts and a T-shirt. Hardy went into the bedroom. There was lipstick on the sheet, but he had no way of knowing if it had been put there last night. He muttered something to himself about having no business messing around with murder and sat down again to wait.

The police finally showed up. First the local precinct, then Homicide. Hardy answered all their questions and left. He knew he was asking for trouble, but he went to see Gerald Friday.

"Hello, Hardy. What do you have for me now? An epidemic?"

"You act as if my main aim in life was to make you miserable."

"Hardy, if you had ever been a real cop you'd know that a cop's life is miserable without anyone trying to make it that way. It just happens."

"You're beginning to sound almost human. Maybe you'll admit that there could be a connection between this killing and Dorothy Robbins."

"Of course there could. There could also be a connection with all the other crimes that happened in the past week. Look, Hardy, the connection is possible. Thank you for drawing it to our attention. Anything else?"

"Did you know Dorothy Robbins was a stripper?"

"Yes."

"Oh. Did you notice that though she had all sorts of glasses for serving liquor, there was no liquor in the place?"

"So?"

"So somebody stole it."

"Or maybe she just ran out. Let me give you a tip. Don't make things complicated. What else?"

"There was lipstick on Leeds' sheet."

"Which means he liked girls. Good-bye, Hardy."

Hardy was very upset as he drove home. He had a few unrelated facts and no conclusions. The end did not seem in sight. He had one consolation though: tonight was the night "The French Chef" was on television.

Chapter Eight

The next day was Saturday. Hardy had planned to spend the morning looking up addresses and phone numbers of the people in the program Leeds had given him. Unfortunately *TV Guide* was on top of the phone book. Jackpot. *The Jolson Story* followed by *If I Were King*. Hardy relegated the list-making to the afternoon and placed the pepperoni, provolone, bread and Pepsi near the TV and prepared to enjoy.

The doorbell rang just as Scotty Becket's voice was changing. Hardy didn't hear the bell, but Holmes did. "Damn it, Holmes. Stop that racket." He opened the apartment door. It was Macker.

"Go away," yelled Hardy. "We don't want any." He turned as if to go back into the apartment. Macker rattled the front door and set Holmes off. The dog kept barking and doing a little dance back and forth in the hall. Hardy yelled at the dog to shut up and let Macker in. Holmes started licking Macker's hand, his tail wagging all the time. "Careful," said Hardy. "My ferocious watch dog may tongue you to death."

They went into the apartment and Hardy turned down the TV. Macker sat down and chewed on a chunk of pepperoni. "Help yourself," said Hardy. "What happened to you? You were supposed to call me yesterday."

"I had to work. I got that commercial I told you about. I miss anything?"

"Yeah. Leeds got killed. He was one of the boy-friends."

"No more kid's games, huh? Sounds like this one's only for grown-ups."

Hardy shooed Holmes away from the cheese and took a wedge for himself. "Don't remind me. Not only is it getting rough, I don't even have an inkling as to who to suspect. I'll go see Vanning, the other boyfriend, on Monday."

"What did you want me for?"

"To trace Vanning for me, but I found him my-self."

Macker went over to the bar. "You're still out of bourbon. You know, the girl might be right."

"How so?"

"Maybe it is an Organization thing!"

"Not you too?"

Macker poured himself some gin. "You got any other ideas?"

Hardy nodded no and turned his attention to the TV. They watched and ate and drank for a while. After Larry Parks finished miming "Rosie," Macker put down his glass and got up. "Take it easy, Pat. You sure have got a stinker."

He walked to the door and turned back to Hardy. "Pat? You own a gun?"

"What do I want with a gun for? I'd probably shoot my toe off. No, I don't own a gun."

"I do. Call me if you need me."

"Yeah. I'll do that."

When Macker left, Hardy had the urgent need to take a shower. His sweat stank so much of fear it made him sick. Afterward he took the phone off the hook and watched television and ate.

He did the same thing on Sunday.

Monday morning he went to see Vanning.

The maid told him to wait. What Hardy could see of the apartment was very elegant. One of the rugs was an Aubusson and the dishes on the Sheraton sideboard looked like very old Dresden. This certainly didn't jibe with Leeds' description of Vanning. Hardy hoped he was in the right place. The maid came back out. "Mr. Vanning would like to know what your visit is in reference to."

"Tell him . . . it's in reference to the D. Robbins' matter."

Hardy turned his attention back to the Dresden. After a while, a voice boomed at him. "You like that stuff?"

Hardy turned around. He had the right man. "Yes, I like it."

"Doesn't do a thing for me. My wife likes it. And I can afford it, so she gets it. Give me modern functional stuff any day."

"Well," said Hardy. "There's a lot to be said for both points of view . . ."

"That's enough of polite conversational crap. Who are you and what do you want?"

"My name's Patrick Hardy. I'm a private detective."

"Yeah?"

"I believe you knew Miss Robbins."

"How much do you want, Hardy?"

"This isn't a shakedown, Mr. Vanning. I just want a little information."

"What if I just throw you out?"

"Then I tell the police and a few reporter friends."

"All right. Start asking your questions. But ask them all now. I don't ever want to see you again after today."

"When was the last time you saw Dorothy Robbins?"

"I don't know. It's been six months, maybe more."

"Can you account for your whereabouts last Sunday night?"

Vanning made a move toward him, then decided to answer the question. "I didn't feel well that night. Drank too much. I went to sleep early."

"Did anyone see you?"

"No, my wife was at our place in Southampton. The maid was off."

"Did you kill Dorothy Robbins, Mr. Vanning?"

"No, goddammit. Now get out of here."

"Where do you want me to go? To the police? The newspapers?"

"All right, you win. But hurry it up. I have to get to the office."

"Tell me how and where you met her."

"About two years ago. She was doing her act in one of those strip joints downtown. After her turn, she came out and started pushing drinks like they all do. I let her push a few my way. I came back a few times after that and we got to know each other."

"How soon after that did you start paying her bills?"

"I ought to break your neck . . . All right, I'm

married, and I was keeping a B-girl I picked up in some joint. But I loved her. I wanted her to have my kids. I would have taken good care of them. My wife's a lady. She also can't have any children. I love my wife. Does that sound strange? I would never ask her for a divorce. Look at those dishes in the case. See how neat and orderly they are. Well, that's how my Edith and her life is. And nothing's going to change that order. Not me, and certainly not you. Why the hell should I kill Dorothy? She was going to give me a son. I was going to adopt him, legally. Give him my name. You jerk! I had what every man dreams of—a lady at home and a swinger outside. And I loved them both. And I would have had a son. He would have had my blood and my name and now it won't happen. Get the hell out of here, Hardy, before I do commit murder."

As Hardy headed out, the maid popped out of another room and got the door for him. "By the way," he said. "I'm supposed to meet Mr. Vanning later at his office, but I forgot the address."

She smiled at him. "Rockefeller Center."

He smiled back. "What's the full name of the firm again?"

"Louis White and Associates."

Hardy's smile was lost in his confusion as she closed the door behind him.

Several thoughts ran through Hardy's mind as he munched on his second hot dog. One was that Joseph Vanning worked for Louis White. Hardy wondered if it was the same Louis White he had seen in the strip joint. Another thought was that the men who were involved with Dorothy Robbins were so visibly shaken by her death. They talked too freely. Hardy

68

understood Leeds telling a stranger about his private love life. It just didn't ring true for Vanning. He didn't seem the type to tell all. Or had he told all? Hardy washed down his mouthful with the last of his root beer and went to a phone booth. He fed the phone a dime and dialed Steve Macker's number.

"Hello."

"Steve?"

"Yeah."

"Pat Hardy. Remember that strip place we were in?"

"Do I? That was the night Ginger . . ."

"This is no time for sexual reminiscing. Remember those two guys I asked you about?"

"You mean White and Pelligrin?"

"That's right."

"What about them?"

"My question exactly. You hinted something about them, but we were busy with other things so I never did get the straight stuff on them."

"Boy, some detective you are! Louis White is supposed to be Mr. Big of the Organization on the Eastern Seaboard. Ben Pelligrin is his number one man and enforcer. Nobody can prove a thing against White. No record on him. He runs a real estate firm as a front. Pelligrin served a little bit for assault, but that was years ago. What's wrong with you? Don't you read the papers? Every other week there's a veiled accusation against White as a manipulator. They never even spell his name out. He's the one they call Mr. W."

"Where is this firm of Louis White's?"

"Some place in Rockefeller Center."

"Thanks, Steve."

He hung up and dialed another number.

69

"Regal Hotel."

"Peg Robbins, please."

"Hello?"

"Peg? This is Pat."

"Oh? You."

"What does that mean?"

"I tried to reach you all weekend. Your phone was always busy. I couldn't even reach your answering service to leave a message, till this morning. I was so upset when I read about Larry Leeds."

"Oh, I didn't think. I forgot it would be in the papers. Where was it?"

"Huh?"

"What page was it on?"

"It was in the back. Just a few lines."

"What did it say?"

"Here, I'll read it to you. 'The body of Larry Leeds, an unemployed actor, was found in his upper West Side apartment last night. The victim was apparently stabbed to death with a pair of scissors. The body was found by Patsy Hardy, also an actor, a friend of the slain man.' There's one more line, but it's all garbled."

"What do you expect? I don't mind the Patsy part, but actor! Ech!"

"Pat, are you all right?"

"Of course I'm all right. Why shouldn't I be?"

"When I read about you finding Larry, and then I couldn't get hold of you . . . I thought something had happened . . . to you, I mean."

"Nah, I'm fine. I'll call you later."

He called his service. The only message was the one Peg had left. He felt good at the thought of her concern. He smiled at what he thought the future might hold and headed toward Rockefeller Center.

While he waited for a light, he spotted a crowd around a man who was selling paper puppets that seemed to move by themselves. Hardy watched for a while, trying to figure out the con. Then he saw him. At the edge of the crowd a character with a transistor was keeping time to the music. He was also manipulating the puppet with a thin thread that ran from the puppet to his fingers. As Hardy walked away he had the strange sensation that he had just thought of something and had immediately forgotten it. It was like trying to hum a song he knew. He could hear the melody in his head, but he couldn't sing it out loud. He racked his brain for a few blocks, but when he nearly got hit by a car that had jumped the light, he gave it up as a lost cause. He lit a cigarette and stopped to peek through the door and ogle the girls going through their gyrations atop the bar in a nudie joint. The one closest to him was particularly intriguing.

"Tough life, this private detective racket."

Hardy turned around and saw the smirking face of Detective Gerald Friday.

"Oh, hello, Friday. This is a treat. I see you and you're talking to me and it isn't even your precinct."

"What the hell. It's my day off. I can waste my time any way I want to." He tightened his lips in a bad imitation of Bogart. "What's the caper, sweetheart?"

"Very funny. Look, are you any closer to whoever killed Dorothy Robbins?"

"We're getting there. You have to remember, we don't just have one case. Last year over five hundred people were killed in this town. A lot of Dorothy Robbinses get killed. We don't use genius like you do.

Just routine and a lot of sweat. Television and movies to the contrary, we solve most of them that way."

"Please, no lectures on your day off."

"Sorry, sweetheart. Where you headed?"

"Rockefeller Center."

"I'll walk with you to 50th Street. What's at Rockefeller Center?"

Hardy took a last fond look at the young ladies on the bar, and he and Friday headed uptown. "None of your business."

"What's with you, Hardy? I thought you were so anxious to work with me. Calling me all the time. Telling me about dead bodies."

"I'm tired of you giving me a hard time about it. I'll handle this by myself."

"Don't be closemouthed with me. If you find anything and don't pass it on, I'll nail you for obstructing justice."

"What's with me he asks. What the hell's with you? First you put me down for bothering you. Now you're threatening to lock me up if I don't come to you with everything I have. You can't have it both ways. Why don't you make up your mind?"

"Look, the simplest thing would be for you to leave this to the professionals. Stop taking your client's money on false pretenses and send her home. Sooner or later we'll catch the nut who did it."

"She prefers sooner, and if you don't mind, this is where we part company. See you around . . . sweetheart."

As he made his way toward the offices of Louis White and Associates, Hardy wondered at Friday being so close at hand. Was he following him? Hardy decided not to take any chances. He went into the NBC Building and took the escalator down to the underground arcade. He wandered around for a while looking for reflections in the shop windows. As a final precaution he cut through the mob in the post office. Satisfied that he wasn't being followed, he headed for his original destination.

The directory downstairs had designated Suite 1735 as the office he was looking for. He went in.

"Yes, sir. May I help you?"

Hardy took in the receptionist's round, sweatered bosom and answered her. "How do you do? My name is Patrick Hardy. I wonder if I could see Mr. White."

"Is he expecting you?"

"No, but . . . uh . . . uh . . . Mr. Vanning suggested I might look him up. Is Mr. Vanning in?"

While the girl checked, Hardy tried to figure out his next move. He had none. Preplanning had never been one of his strong points. His only hope was that Vanning would be unavailable. As he waited for the girl he fervently regretted being involved in a murder. He wished he had taken the Civil Service examination instead of trying to be a detective. He wished he wasn't where he was. At last he decided the best thing to do would be to leave. He turned to the door . . .

"Mr. White will see you now."

"What?"

"I said Mr. White will see you now. Mr. Vanning isn't in at the moment, but Mr. White has some free time and will be glad to see you."

"Thank you."

Another pretty girl came out and led him into Louis White's office. "Come in, Mr. Hardy."

Ben Pelligrin was with him.

"This is my associate, Mr. Pelligrin. Now then, this

73

is very unusual, no appointment and all that. But any friend of Mr. Vanning's . . ."

"Actually," said Hardy, "I was in the building and I saw your name and thought as long as I was here it wouldn't hurt to try."

"Of course," said White. "Of course. What can I do for you?"

Hardy hadn't the slightest idea what he could tell White he could do for him. "Well," he said, and he lit a cigarette. The cigarette didn't give him any inspiration. All he could think of was that he knew Ben Pelligrin from somewhere. Since that's what he was thinking, that's what he said.

"Excuse me, Mr. Pelligrin, but have we ever met?"

Pelligrin was very pleasant. "No, I don't think so." Suddenly the pleasantness disappeared. "Maybe you saw me the night you started that ruckus in the club."

Louis White shook his head. "There you go spoiling it, Ben. You just have no patience. Now we'll never know what subterfuge Mr. Hardy would have invented to justify his visit here. You should remember that, Mr. Hardy. Ben has no patience. You really are an amateur, aren't you?"

Hardy decided against bluffing. "Yes, I really am."

"Good. At least you know that much. There's hope for you yet. As it stands, there's no reason for you to be here, Mr. Hardy. I don't even want to know why you think you're here. From this moment on you have nothing to do with me and mine. My business is none of your business. Good-bye, Mr. Hardy."

To make matters worse, as Hardy left the office, he ran into Joseph Vanning coming in. "Hardy, what the hell are you doing here?"

74

"I forgot to ask you before, Mr. Vanning. Where were you Friday night about three A.M.? That was the night Larry Leeds was killed. Well, I see you're very busy, Mr. Vanning. Perhaps another time. Goodbye."

When he got home, his answering service told him a Mrs. Bushman had called. He dialed the number she had left.

"Hello."

"Mrs. Bushman?"

"This is Tilly Bushman."

"My name is Patrick Hardy. You called me."

"Oh, yes. I wanted to tell you who killed that girl. You know, Robbins."

"Who?"

"Amanda Delaney did it, that's who."

"How do you know this, Mrs. Bushman?"

"I live in the next building. I know a lot of things."

"But how do you know Amanda Delaney killed Dorothy Robbins?"

"Oh, was that her first name? I used to know it, but I forgot. Amanda hated that girl. That girl didn't do right by her."

"How do you know she killed her?"

"I saw her do it."

"You mean you were there?"

"Of course not. I was home in bed the night it happened. I don't go galavanting about at night. I'm at home where I ought to be. I saw it last night . . . in a dream."

"Mrs. Bushman, how did you get my name and number?"

"Oh, that nice policeman, Mr. Friday, gave it to me. He was too busy to talk to me, but he said you wouldn't be too busy, and that you would love to talk to me. So he gave me your number."

"Wasn't that nice of him?"

"Yes."

"Mrs. Bushman?"

"Yes."

"Do you know Detective Friday's home number?"

"No, I don't."

"Well, today is his day off. And I'm sure with a name like Gerald Friday, it shouldn't be too hard for you to get his number from information."

"Do you think I should?"

"I'm positive. He's always so lonely for someone to talk to on his day off. I'm sure he'll appreciate it."

"I'll do that right now. Good-bye, Mr. Hardy."

"Good-bye."

Hardy considered looking up Friday's number himself and calling Mrs. Bushman back. While he was pondering this, the phone rang again.

"Hello, Mr. Hardy. Tilly Bushman here. I got the number like you said."

"That's wonderful, Mrs. Bushman."

"I thought you might like to have it."

"No, Mrs. Bushman. You use it."

"Take it down. You never know when you'll need it."

Hardy finally took the number down to get rid of her. It didn't work. He had to put up with five more minutes of aimless conversation before she hung up. After a glass of vegetable juice, he leashed up Holmes and went out into the park. While Holmes romped, Hardy leafed through the afternoon paper to see if some smart newspaperman had done some of his work for him. No such luck. He decided to call the day a bust and was just about to throw the paper away when he spotted an ad proclaiming that Ruby Red was the star attraction in a burlesque house in Forest Hills. He told himself the only reason he was going to see her was because Milly had told him she knew Dorothy Robbins.

After White's warning, Hardy didn't think it would be good for him to be recognized visiting Ruby Red. Besides, he liked disguises. Surprisingly enough the disguises Hardy chose to use were rather effective—because they were so simple. Hardy was a foolish man, but he wasn't dumb.

He went back into the house and got to work. With the aid of some pomade he slicked his hair down. A little cotton under his upper lip changed the contour of his mouth. A pair of thick-rimmed glasses with plain glass and a Band-Aid across his cheek completed the picture. Satisfied with his handiwork, he undid it and took a nap. And dreamed about Ruby Red . . .

When he awoke, Hardy took a shower, fed Holmes and fried a steak for himself. He changed his greasy pillowcase and then redid his disguise, put on a baggy tweed suit, hopped in his car and headed for Forest Hills.

Traffic was fairly light over the 59th Street Bridge, and as he drove along Hardy found himself daydreaming about an idea he had for the car. One of these days he was going to put a Porsche engine in his VW. He had read about Paul Newman doing it, and it seemed like a good idea. Hardy got so involved in how he was going to fake out everybody in his speedy Volks that he almost missed the turn-off for the Long Island Expressway.

There were no spaces in front of the theater so he drove a couple of blocks away and parked. He had planned on seeing Ruby Red after the show, but he was early and, rather than kill time in a bar, he elected to try to see her before. The usual old man was guarding the stage door.

"Yeah. What do you want?"

Hardy put on his best fey attitude. "I'd like to see Ruby Red, please. I'm a writer."

"A lot of guys want to see her. But I think you'd be a new one on her. Wait here. I'll ask."

While Hardy waited for the doorman to check, he looked around. Two strippers in robes and nothing else were talking together. Of course Hardy forgot his characterization and stared hard.

"What the hell are you looking at, four-eyes?" The stevedore voice came out of the bigger of the two strippers. Hardy remembered what he was supposed to be.

"Nothing at all, sweetie."

"If that don't beat it. Now the fags are coming to burlesque."

Hardy managed to pout and look hurt. The tough stripper kept talking to her companion. "Come on, Monica. I probably got one bigger than he has." Toughie then put a protective arm over Monica's shoulder and swaggered off in her best bull-dyke manner. By this time the doorman was back.

"She'll see you. In the back there. Her name's on the door." Hardy crossed to the door designated and knocked.

"Come in."

She was bending over and maneuvering her breasts into what looked to be a too-small bra. "Be with you in a minute. I want to finish getting dressed so I can relax a minute." Hardy was certainly not relaxed. The reaction of his body was definitely not that of the

78

gay fellow he was pretending to be. She finished her fastening and sat down to work on her hair.

"Herbie didn't tell me your name."

"I'm . . . Edgar Paisley. And I'm doing a book about stripteasers and the life they live. If you wouldn't mind answering a few questions, I'd be very appreciative."

She looked him over, particularly the spot below his belt.

"Why not? Have a seat."

She smiled as he moved away some filmy underwear from the seat she offered.

"Now. My book concerns itself more with the backstage life than the actual work. The day-to-day existence of a stripper. What she does. What she has to put with."

"Sounds good."

"For instance, when a girl works in a club, does she have to mix?"

"You sure you want to write this book?"

"Yes. Why not?"

"Well, it sounds like you're trying to write an exposé, and frankly, you don't look the type."

"Oh, no. I'd never write anything like that. More like a sympathetic comment on the terrible life some girls are forced to lead."

"Crap. Nobody forces you. What the hell is wrong with stripping? It's a good life. I have a great body, and I like to show it off."

"You must admit that most of the girls in the business hate men."

"Oh, we have some dykes and like that. And we can't stand most of the creeps who come to gawk. But most of us are pretty healthy. We like getting laid."

"Oh. Oh, me. What about all those men in the clubs who manhandle the girls that are drinking with them?"

"That's a bad part of it, I admit that. But I don't mix, so it doesn't bother me. That *is* pretty creepy."

"Do most of the girls have to mix?"

"Oh, yeah. Until you get some sort of a name—even then for some. That's part of the deal. That's why I'm glad to see burlesque houses opening again. You get paid to strip, and that's it. You don't have to hustle all night to see how many bottles of phony champagne you can sell."

Hardy took out his notebook and pretended to look something up. "Do you know a stripper called Milly?"

"I know a few."

"Well, the one I talked to said you might be able to help me in one area. Following up on my theory that stripping is a harsh life, I'm trying to get some information on a stripper who was killed last week. Dorothy Robbins. Milly said you knew her."

Ruby laughed. As she did Hardy watched her breasts trying to escape from their confinement.

"Wait a minute," said Ruby, "I get it now. Did this Milly have a friend named Ginger?"

"Yes, I believe she did."

"Well, she must have thought there was something fishy about you. She steered you wrong in order to protect Ginger. Dotty Robbins was Ginger's pal, not mine. You better beat it now. I have to go to work. Why don't you come back after the show? We'll have a drink."

Hardy minced a bit. "Well. . . ."

"You can cut out that fag act too. I can tell a man

80

when I see one. My equipment starts certain reactions, and you reacted."

Hardy relaxed. "O.K., I thought it would be easier to see you this way."

"Sure . . . sure. Lose those glasses and wipe that gook out of your hair too. You have a reputation to live up to, Mr. Hardy. Milly told me all about you. She says you're good in bed." She walked over to him and ripped the Band-Aid from his cheek. "See you later."

Hardy decided to leave the rest of his disguise in place and went out front and bought a ticket. Most of the acts were run-of-the-mill. A couple of baggy-pants comics were very funny with an old bit called "Flugel Street." The lesbian Hardy had talked to backstage did a surprisingly feminine act. Not bad either. But Ruby was what he was waiting for. She closed the show with her swan act. It was toned down some from the way she had presented it in the club, but it was still stimulating. His mouth grew so dry he had to throw away the cotton. When the show let out, he smoked a cigarette and waited in order to give the crowd backstage a chance to dwindle. After a while he went to Ruby's dressing room.

"Hi, I'll be ready in a minute. Hand me that dress, will you?"

Hardy thought he adjusted to all the shocks Ruby had caused his glands. Not so. She was wearing panties and bra, but the bra was transparent and the panties were almost nonexistent. Seeing Ruby close-up in see-through clothing stimulated him all over again. She winked at him. "Pretty good, huh?"

He nodded.

"Hey," she said. "I thought you were going to get that junk out of your hair."

Hardy wiped the sweat from his forehead. "I thought I'd wait till we got to your place."

"Pretty sure of yourself, aren't you? Here, I'll do it for you." She put her dress on a chair and grabbed a towel and took off his glasses. "Lean over the sink." With face soap and hot water and a lot of brisk rubbing she got most of the pomade out. He could feel her and smell her while she worked. When she was done, he stood up and she took a comb from her table and combed his hair. She stood in front of him, combing, smiling, pushing and teasing. He put his hands on her breasts and pulled her to him and kissed her.

"About friggin' time," she said. "If there's one thing I can't stand, it's a gentleman."

When he got a little more frantic she pushed him away. "Steady, lover. I'm not about to make it in some crumby dressing room. Besides," she pouted, "I'm not that easy. First you'll have to feed me and buy me a few drinks, and be nice to me."

He took another nibble of her lips and released her. "Come on. My car's a couple of blocks from here."

He never got to his car. As they walked out of the theater, someone sapped him just behind the ear. His reflexes didn't even have a chance to reflex. He should never have removed his disguise, or had Ruby . . . ?

He was back in the barber shop again. But he wasn't fat. He was lean and hungry. The man without a face was going to shoot him in the stomach. He heard the shot. He felt the pain. The man without a face was coming closer. He was bending over to look at him. For the first time Hardy seemed to see a face where there never had been one before. If only he would come a little closer . . . just a little closer . . .

"Hey, buddy. If the cops find you sleeping there, they'll kick your ass."

82

As Hardy got to his feet the drunk who had given him the advice slumped to the ground and took over Hardy's sleeping spot. Hardy walked away from the stage door and toward the entrance of the alley. He started to feel woozy and leaned against a wall. He threw up, then wiped his mouth and lit a cigarette. A look at his watch told him that he had been out for over an hour. As he started for the VW he heard the clack of high heels on the sidewalk. It was Ruby. She rushed toward him. "Gee, you look awful. I'm so glad you're all right. They made me get in a car with them, and they dumped me in Manhattan. I couldn't get a cab. I finally had to take the subway. Are you all right?"

Hardy spit in the gutter. "Go to hell Ruby."

"Wait a minute. You don't think I had anything to do with this, do you? Why would I come all the way back to see if you were all right?"

"See you around, Ruby."

"Come on. Use your head. If I had anything to do with it, would I have come back? Come on, I'll take you to my place. You'll feel better."

By this time he was at his car. He got in. "No thanks, Ruby. If there was another reception waiting for me like the one I got here, I'd never forgive myself. Nice knowing you." He slammed the door and took off as fast as is possible in a Volkswagen.

"Hey," yelled Ruby. "How am I going to get home? Screw you," she said to nobody in particular and headed for the subway.

Chapter Nine

When Hardy woke the next morning, his mouth and nose and throat responded to the irritations offered by Con Edison and other sundry people who do business in the city of New York. After hacking for a while he gargled and swore off cigarettes . . . again. He picked up *Before the Deluge* from the night table and read a chapter. Finally he crawled out of the king-sized bed and checked himself in the mirror. His friends from the night before had kindly left his face alone, but they hadn't been that kind to his kidneys. He soaked in a hot tub to ease the pain and forced himself to go through a workout. After a shower, he had a large bowl of grapenuts and applesauce and he felt a little better. He got dressed and walked Holmes, then decided to call Peg.

Just as he was lifting the phone to dial, the doorbell rang. It was probably the maid, but yesterday's incident made him a little cautious. He looked out the barred window and resolved to get a TV hook-up for the hall as soon as he had the money.

She was probably the most beautiful woman he had ever seen. He quickly checked himself in the mirror and started for the door. He stopped and looked out the window again. She seemed to be alone. Hardy told Holmes to shut up and rushed to let her in.

He felt hypnotized as he led this tall blonde piece of perfection into his office.

"Mr. Hardy, my name is Vivica Johnson. I need your help."

"Well, Miss Johnson, I'm on a case right now, but perhaps I can be of service."

"Please, you must help me. This won't take much of your time. I'm being blackmailed."

"I see," said Hardy. "Well, that's a bit out of my line, and as I said before, I am on a case now."

She got up and crossed to his side of the desk and touched his arm. "Please, Mr. Hardy. I need your help. And I would be so grateful."

"Well . . ."

"Please, I know it's early, but might I have something to drink?"

"Of course. What'll it be?"

"A little sherry, please."

He poured the sherry for her and one for himself, even though he hated the stuff. Their hands brushed as he gave her her drink. Hardy's libido had been frustrated the night before and this new experience wasn't helping him. She sipped her drink and sat on the chaise and crossed her legs. Hardy started to walk back to his desk. Her proximity would be too devastating at the moment.

"Please, Mr. Hardy. Sit with me. Even if you can't help me, I must tell someone."

It was a suspicious setup, but his gonads got in the way of his cerebrum and he didn't notice. He went to the chaise. "How can I help you?"

"You must help me in buying back some photographs. If my husband ever sees them, my life will be ruined."

Her mentioning a husband seemed to dampen things a bit, but not much. He needed an excuse to walk around.

"Excuse me a minute."

He got up and walked to the hall and checked to see if the police lock was engaged. He took a deep breath and came back to his office. "You were talking about your husband."

"Yes. We live in Sweden. I am here on holiday. Alone. My husband is very rich. He is also very vain. If he ever found out what certain photographs prove, he would surely kill me."

"And what do they prove?"

She licked her lips and pulled him down on the chaise. "That I am a nymphomaniac."

He was dreaming of breasts and lips and thighs. Somewhere in the distance he heard Holmes barking. He opened his eyes and saw the bloody knife. He couldn't move. He was fascinated by the knife, by its ornate handle and its intricate push-button mechanism, but mostly by its blood. The stiletto rested on the pillow, along with a small package. Vivica was gone. Then he felt the stickiness on his side. Some more blood. His pulse accelerated, and he found it very hard to swallow as he examined the wound. It was just a scratch. A very deliberate scratch in the shape of a W.

After he washed the blood away and bandaged his wound, Hardy reconnoitered the apartment. Holmes dogged his footsteps and barked again as Hardy looked about. "Shut up. Where were you when I needed you?"

He went back to the bedroom and put on his pants. Covering his nakedness made him feel a little less vulnerable.

Hardy cleaned the stiletto and closed it. He winced as the powerful spring sent the blade back into the handle. He opened the package. There were a lot of twenty-dollar bills and a note.

"Dear Mr. Hardy:

I hope you have enjoyed yourself. V. is a very remarkable woman. She works for me. You will find that a lot of people work for me.

Forgive the overelaborateness and melodrama . . . but it does make my point. . . . YOU ARE ASSAILABLE.

Accept my apologies for last night. Those men work for me, but I'm afraid they overstepped themselves. I am beyond that sort of thing. Believe me, if I want to inflict punishment, it will be nothing so crude as a beating.

I'd rather appeal to your other weaknesses. And, Mr. Hardy, you have many.

The woman and the money are to appeal to your lustful and venal nature.

The knife and the scratch is a reminder of what will happen if you don't stay bought.

You are very assailable, Mr. Hardy. Don't make me prove it permanently. Stay out of my affairs.

W.

W. was right. Hardy did have many weaknesses, but the one W. didn't reckon on was pride. If well enough had been left alone, Hardy probably would have given up the case after the beating of the night before and gone back to trailing errant husbands and finding lost dogs. But W. had attacked him where he was most sensitive: his fear syndrome. He had made Hardy come face to face with his fear. The confrontation hurt his pride and made him angry.

He called a bonded messenger and rewrapped the package. He addressed it to Louis White at his Rockefeller Center office. As an afterthought, he pasted one of his cards to the package and scrawled a little note: "Dear Mr. White, screw you." And he signed it. H.

The Messenger had just gone. Hardy was tempted to call him back, but his pride was stronger than his fear. He wondered if he would regret it. Then his thoughts drifted to Vivica Johnson's body and his tactile memory of it and he smiled. He was about to review the whole sexual episode when the doorbell rang. Hardy tensed up and furtively looked out the window. He relaxed. It was only the maid.

"Hello, Mr. Hardy, the doorman gave me this mail for you."

"Thanks, Laura."

While she got busy, Hardy looked it over. Besides some bills and junk mail there was a letter for Dorothy Robbins that had been forwarded to him. It turned out to be an announcement that Bonwit's was having a sale. But at least he knew that one of his plans was functioning.

In a moment of anger he had kept himself on the case; however, the anger had dissipated, and though he wanted to get at it, he wasn't up to tackling White and his group at that moment. He thought back to Tilly Bushman's call. Although he didn't give much credence to her accusation of Amanda Delaney, it was a lead and it had to be eliminated. And it was safe.

Hardy finished getting dressed and walked to

Amanda Delaney's building. He expected to run into the cigarette fiend he had met the last time. Luckily he wasn't there. Hardy hoped he had been murdered.

He identified the smells in the hallway as perfume and chicken soup and rang Amanda Delaney's bell.

"Who is it?"

"Taking a poll, ma'am."

She continued talking to him through the door. "What kind of poll?"

Hardy cast about in his mind for a second. "We are trying to determine . . . uh . . . what . . . uh, liquor is the most popular."

By this time she was peering at him through the space allowed her by the chain-lock. "Do I get anything?"

"Yes, ma'am. If your favorite liquor is on our list, we send you a bottle."

"What if it's not on the list?"

"Then we send you one that is."

"O.K. Ask away."

"Aren't you going to open up?"

"You can ask from where you are."

Hardy chewed on his lip. "No thank you, ma'am. My feet hurt. I'm not going to conduct any interview standing out in the hall. I'll try the next apartment."

She unhooked the chain. "Wait a minute. I guess you're O.K."

Cats. All over the place. He guessed there were at least six. It smelled like a hundred.

She pointed him to a couch. "Don't step on any of my babies." As if on cue, a real baby started crying in the next room. She grunted something at him and went into the next room. He heard some cooing noises, and then the baby was quiet. She came back in, and almost as a reflex action, she reached for one

89

of the many liquor bottles that were in the dry sink she used as a bar. She pulled her hand away when she saw Hardy watching her. Then in a to-hell-with-you manner she grabbed for some Scotch and poured herself a shot. Hardy got up and crossed over to the dry sink. She was a large woman. Her hair was a lot of different shades of brown. Hardy figured her to be 55 or so. She sipped her drink very delicately. Her eyes never left him. He looked over the array of opened bottles. That was strange. There were two Schenleys open. Two Teachers and several other brands with two bottles opened. He was about to comment when . . . .

"Haven't I seen you someplace before?"

She had remembered him from the brief look she had had of him that day in the hall. He mentally kicked himself. Of all times not to think of some sort of disguise. He ignored her question. "Well from what I see here you certainly qualify for the bonus bottle. Do you live alone here?"

"Why?"

"That's one of the questions I'm supposed to ask."

"I live alone. I'm watching the baby for my daughter. You have any other questions?"

"No, I can fill in the rest for myself."

For no explainable reason Hardy felt a desperate need to get out of there. Some sort of basic panic set in. He wasn't afraid of her per se, but something about her apartment was menacing. "Well, thank you very much. I'll see you get the liquor."

As he reached for the knob, she cried, "You're no poll taker. I remember. . . ."

He didn't wait to find out what she did remember. He slammed the door and took the stairs down.

The doorman filled him in a bit on Amanda. She

90

wasn't married so that child was not her daughter's. She baby-sat for most of the building and would board a baby for a while if necessary. The doorman couldn't tell him anything about Amanda and Dot Robbins since he was new in the building. Hardy gave him a dollar and went home.

His service told him to call Gerald Friday.

"Point one," said the cop, when Hardy reached him. "Thanks for giving Tillie Bushman the idea of calling me at home. I needed that."

"Anything to repay a favor," Hardy told him.

"Point two. Amanda Delaney, a woman who lives across the hall from Dorothy Robbins' apartment, as I'm sure you know, just called. Boy, some detective you are! You can't even question a subject without her tumbling. She called here and said she was being harassed. She described you. Don't bother to deny it, my man watching the house saw you, too."

"*Mea culpa*. Shall I turn myself in?"

"Don't be wise with me, Hardy. Just stop causing me sweat."

He had just hung up the phone when it started ringing again. He picked it up. "Hello."

"Jesus. What were you doing? Sitting on it? It's me, Steve. I'm having a bash at my place tonight. Why don't you come over?"

"Sure. Should I bring a date?"

"Do you bring sandwiches to a banquet?"

"What time?"

"Any time after nine."

After Hardy hung up, he brushed the cat hairs from his suit and made a grilled cheese sandwich. Then he turned on the TV.

Chapter Ten

Macker lived in an old brownstone on 81st Street just a few blocks away from Hardy. Hardy had planned to saunter over about nine, but he got hooked on a Glenn Ford movie. And, of course, while he watched he had to eat. Finally, at eleven, he lit an after-snack cigarette and headed toward 81st Street.

If the sounds he heard on the street were any indication, it was a great party. Hardy climbed over couples that were littering the halls and made his way to the second floor. He didn't have to knock, the door was open, which was logical since the party seemed to be in the whole building and not just in Macker's apartment. As usual, there were mobs and bobs of humanity, most of it feminine. Macker always stacked a party in his favor.

Hardy pushed to where the liquor was, poured himself a Scotch and started cruising. The Scotch was too heavy for his taste, but it was too much trouble to go back to the bar, so he drank it anyway. That was a mistake. It gave him instant indigestion. He parked the empty glass and searched for food to ease his stomach. After he did in some onion dip, he started cruising again.

"Pat, over here." It was Macker with the most fascinatingly ugly girl Hardy had ever seen. Her figure was full and well formed but her face was all crags. Despite this, she was very sexy, sort of an ugly Raquel Welch.

Macker grinned at him. "Paula Marx, Pat Hardy. Pat Hardy, Paula Marx."

The girl lifted her hand in greeting. Macker patted her on the behind. "Beat it for a while, honey, I want to talk to this character. Besides, if you stay around, he's liable to tear your clothes off right here."

Paula pouted at being dismissed. Macker turned to Hardy. "Doesn't she have great boobs?"

She glowed at the compliment and wiggled into the crowd. They both watched her go, and then Macker said, "Well, Pat. How's it going?"

"It doesn't go, I have to push it. Joke over. Lots of brick walls, Steve. Let's forget it. Maybe I'll get drunk. Maybe I'll get laid. Odds are I won't feel better in the morning, but at least I'll have a new slant on things."

Just then Hardy saw a familiar face. "Hey, isn't that . . . ?"

Macker nodded. "I forgot to tell you. I called Ginger up and told her to come over with some of her friends. You ought to try some of that. It ain't bad."

"Hello, Pat." Hardy looked up. Another familiar face. Ruby Red.

"Hi, Ruby." He turned to Macker. "What did you

93

do? Invite the who's who of burlesque? Ruby Red, Steve Macker. Steve Macker, Ruby Red."

Macker admired Ruby a bit and then lit a cigarette. "Well, Pat old buddy, this looks like it's going to be a good party. See you both later." Macker moved off, and Hardy tried to spot Ginger. Ruby touched his arm. "What are you trying to do, Pat, ignore me?"

"Give the lady a cigar. Right on the first try."

"I ought to break your neck."

"If not you, one of your playmates will."

"Pat, what do I have to do to convince you that I'm not hooked up with those creeps?"

"Look, I believe you. Now can I go?"

"If you'll only let me talk to you for a few minutes."

"And while you do that, what happens to Ginger? Is that the bit? Yeah, that's it. For some reason you don't want me to talk to Ginger. Or you don't want her to talk to me. What happened? Couldn't you stop her from coming here? Sure, that's it. It figured that I'd be here. And when they couldn't stop her, they sent you along to stop me."

"I don't know what you're talking about."

"Cut it out, will you? You're more convincing when you're taking off your clothes." Hardy turned back to the crowd.

Ruby flushed and let loose with a round-house right that made his ear ring. "Thanks," he said. "I needed that." He walked off and looked for Ginger.

He found her off in a corner. She was feeling no pain. He sat down next to her.

"Hi, Ginger."

"Hi. Hey, do I know you? Yeah, I know you. You're Steve's friend." She took another pull at the bottle she had. "Milly told me you were asking about Dotty. Dotty was a sweet kid. Why should anyone want to hurt Dotty? I don't know why. Yes, I do. I know why. You know why?"

"Why what? To hell with that. Let's dance."

She carefully stashed the bottle in the corner of the couch. "Keep your eye on that. Come on, let's dance."

She threw her arms about Hardy's neck and pressed herself to him. He pretended to dance to the music he couldn't hear.

"What about Dotty, Ginger? Why would anyone want to kill her?"

"I'll tell you later. You can take me home. Now let's dance."

They rubbed bodies for a while, and Hardy tried to figure his next move. If he took her out now, someone might be watching the building.. He had to talk to her here. He remembered that there was an empty room upstairs.

"Ginger . . . why don't you and I . . ."

It felt like he'd been hit in the chest with a sledge-hammer. He couldn't figure it out. He looked down and Ginger . . . that's when he saw the blood separating them. He let go of her in horror. Her body slumped, but her hands were in a death lock around his neck. The blood was gushing so that her breast looked like a macabre gourd pouring wine. Frantically he unlocked her fingers and let her down.

Somebody noticed finally and started yelling. "Hey, not here, take her to a bedroom." This seemed very funny to the yeller, and he started laughing.

Hardy grabbed the man and shook him. "She's been shot, you clown. Somebody call an ambulance . . . and call the cops." This wasn't a good move on

95

Hardy's part. Not everyone believed him, but those who did started for the door in an attempt to get out before the police arrived. Hardy calmed himself down. He spotted Macker. "Steve, call an ambulance."

When he was sure Macker understood him, he started searching for the source of the shot. He hadn't heard anything, but the noise in the apartment had been deafening. By this time others were trying to get out. He stood up on a chair and yelled.

"Goddamn it! Everybody stop." Everybody stopped. He had that kind of voice. "I don't blame you. I'd like to get out of here myself. But if the cops find out you were here and took off, you'll be in a lot of trouble. So just cool it and stick around." Much to Hardy's surprise, they nodded at him while some mumbled that he was right and went back to their drinking. He shook his head in wonderment at his success and went back to Ginger. There was a large empty space around her. No one had gone to see if they could help. The blood had stopped gushing. She was dead. Hardy grabbed a rug and covered her. While everyone continued partying he tried to remember how he and Ginger had been standing. The door. He had been looking at the door. The hallway. The shot must have been fired from the hallway. He went out there. No luck. No ejected cartridge case on the floor. No witnesses. All the hallway lovers had gone off to more comfortable locations. Macker followed him out. "I called the cops. Pat, this is getting rougher and rougher."

"Very astute observation." The pain in his chest was worse.

"Hey, this is no time to get cute," Macker told him. "These guys have declared open season on people, and you might be next. Pat, what's wrong with you?"

"I have a funny feeling you're right. I think I've been shot too." And he collapsed.

Chapter Eleven

He was running, and the man without a face was chasing him. Hardy couldn't move. There was a string tied to his leg. Somebody was manipulating him like a paper puppet. He looked for the other end of the string. It was tied around the waist of a nude woman. Every time she moved, he had to move. He couldn't see her face either. The man without a face was coming closer. He tried to run but couldn't. The woman kept manipulating her body, and his movements were subject to hers. He tried to see her face. His eyes kept being drawn to her breasts. They were growing larger and larger. He tore his eyes away and focused on her face. In a minute he would be able to see her face. Just a little closer. The breasts were growing still larger. Now they were obscuring her face. Now the man was coming closer.

"Come on, Pat. Snap out of it."

Hardy opened his eyes and saw Steve Macker grinning at him. "Come on. Nap time is over."

He adjusted the focus of his eyes so that he could make out the other people. There was Ruby . . . and Gerald Friday . . . and a lot of busy men doing a lot of busy things. His chest hurt. He was on the couch where he had talked to Ginger. As his memory came back, Hardy looked down at the floor. No Ginger. Just blood stains and chalk marks to indicate where she had been. His chest bothered him again. Somebody had taken off his shirt. A man who looked like a doctor came over and prodded him where the pain was. He winced and looked down at his chest. No wound, a large black-and-blue mark.

The doctor type wrinkled his forehead and said, "You're a very lucky man. The bullet went through her and hit the pen you had in your pocket. It'll be sore for a while, but that's all." He wrinkled his forehead some more and walked away.

Friday walked over to the couch. "That's a nice color you have there, Hardy. A decided improvement. You can go home now if you want to, but I want you in my office tomorrow morning."

"Hello, Friday. What are you doing up so late? I thought you were a strictly nine-to-five cop."

"Overtime. Do me a favor. Go straight home. Everywhere you are there seems to be trouble." He turned to Ruby. "You can leave anytime you want, Miss. All right, Macker, let's have another try at those names."

As Friday and Macker went into the next room, Hardy could hear Macker protesting, "Honest, I don't know half the people who were here, and those I do know, I only know by their first names."

Hardy looked quizzically at Ruby.

She smiled. "When you passed out, everybody decided to ignore your advice and leave."

Hardy reached for his shirt, but she grabbed it and helped him put it on.

"All right," he said. "I give up. Why did you stick around?"

"The police wanted to talk to me."

"Besides that."

"I thought I'd take another try at convincing you that I'm on your side."

"Despite what happened to Ginger?"

"Despite what happened to Ginger."

He sucked his teeth for a moment. Then he looked at her. That clinched it. She certainly looked like the kind of friend he'd like to have. "Oh, I'm a jerk, but I believe you. But just to be on the safe side, I'll put you on probation."

She faked a swing at him. "Why you . . ."

"Take care. I'm a wounded man. Why don't you walk me home?"

"That sounds nice."

Hardy put on his jacket and shoved his tie in his pocket. They said good night to Macker and Friday who said good night back to them in an all-knowing manner, and they went out into the street.

He took her arm as they walked downtown. Hardy thought of a lot of things to say but rejected them. Instead, he took silent pleasure in the pressure of her breast against his arm as they walked. His pulse started racing as he closed the front door to his apartment. Impatiently, he pounced on her. As she returned his embrace, he yelled in pain and suddenly he was very dizzy and not at all in the mood for sex.

"Oh, Pat. I'm sorry. I didn't think about your chest."

"I've been thinking about yours."

"Very funny. I think we'd better wait."

"Don't be silly. Come on in."

"Oh no, lover. The first time with you I want you to be in condition. Call me. 240-1112." Her lips brushed his, and she was gone.

Hardy went inside and straight to bed. He wasn't alone. He had Holmes for company.

Chapter Twelve

On Wednesday Hardy skipped his workout and had a double breakfast.

He sorted clothes for the cleaners, including the jacket he had worn the night before. While he was wondering if the cleaner would be able to remove the blood stain, he felt something hard in the top pocket. He fished in and brought out a gnarled piece of lead that had been a bullet. He whistled at it and put it in an envelope to give to Friday. He called Ruby but she wasn't in. He left a message with her service. Then he called Peg, but she wasn't in either, so he left another message. He tried to watch some game shows on TV, but there was no getting away from it—sooner or later he had to go and see Friday.

Hardy ignored his car and walked over to Broadway and got on the subway. Rush hour was over, but it was crowded enough to make him nervous. It was only one stop, but the thought of all those people packed tighter than any humane society would allow cattle to be packed always made him itchy, and the events of the last few days had made him more susceptible than ever to his little phobias. He jumped at the repeated thumping sound as several people released their overhead hand straps . . . then the chewers joined in. The dozens of jaws noisily chomping their spearmint and juicy fruit. He was a wreck. The noises and the chewers and the many noxious mouths and armpits that surrounded him were too much. 79th Street. He got off. That is, he tried to get off. As the door opened, fellow New Yorkers thronged on without giving anyone a chance to get off. Hardy girded himself and pushed through the oncoming mass muttering, "Let 'em off. First let 'em off, then you get on."

Paying no attention to the looks of the crowd, he ran up the stairs. He sat on a bench and smoked a few cigarettes to calm down and passed the time watching the junkies go by. After a while he went into a bar and had a beer. He tasted it, left the rest and walked out. Hardy hated beer. He thought about leaving town and forgetting the whole mess but decided that that wouldn't work.

Quickly, before he could change his mind, he hailed a passing cab and rode the few remaining blocks to the police station. He overtipped the puzzled cabbie and went in.

Hardy asked the officer at the desk if Gerald Friday was in. The officer pointed to the staircase he had used the last time he had been there. Hardy paused at the sign that pointed to the squad room. After examining all the fly specks on the arrow, he lit another cigarette and read the sign that told him that the detectives were on the second floor, and the PAL was on the third floor, and that a Civil Defense office was on the fourth floor. He meandered into the squad room and read a few wanted posters. Then he looked over a large chart which identified the precinct's target for the week and showed a picture of an inoffensive-looking man who was dubbed an habitual gambler. Finally, after running out of reading material, he went up to the second floor where he knew Friday's office was. Friday didn't seem to be around. Hardy watched a detective showing two others how to tie a knot in a rope using one hand. Friday came out of the toilet and into the office. Hardy saw him enter and crossed over to his desk. Friday interrupted him.

"Before you say it. No, that's not all they have to do. Like everyone else we goof off once in a while. We are human."

Friday glanced angrily at the three detectives who were fiddling with the rope and then turned his attention back to Hardy.

"All right. Let's have it."

"It all ties in with Dot Robbins and Larry Leeds."

Friday groaned. "Look, don't complicate things for me. Tell me what you know about the girl and what your connection with her was."

Hardy pulled out the envelope with the piece of lead. "Present for you. I found it in my pocket, believe it or not. Must have fallen there after it hit my pen. I don't know what ballistics can do with it, but it is evidence."

The black cop tore open the envelope and looked at the slug. "It's just like everything else I get from you, Hardy. All distorted and unusable."

"Very clever wordplay," Hardy said.

"Thanks for nothing. Now, let's have it."

"Her name is Ginger . . . I don't know her last name."

Friday glanced at the folder in his hand. "Her name was Marlene Povnick. She worked under the name of Ginger Peach. Go on, you're doing great."

"First time I ever saw her was last week, in some dump. I forget the name. Macker knows it."

The cop smiled. He was enjoying himself. "It's called the Cornucopia Club."

"Anyway, I didn't know it when I met her, but she knew Dot Robbins, who we know was also a stripper. Last night was the first time I had seen her since last week. In the interim I have been in contact with two gentlemen whom you might know. Mr. Louis White and Mr. Ben Pelligrin. As a matter of fact, I saw them the day I ran into you. Or where you there on purpose?"

Friday rubbed his mustache and waited for Hardy to continue.

"Anyway," said Hardy, "I can't prove it, but I think there's a connection between my nosing around about Dot Robbins and Ginger getting killed. I think that connection is Louis White and Ben Pelligrin. I don't think they wanted Ginger to talk to me . . . I also saw them at the Cornucopia Club."

"Anything else?"

"I don't think so."

"What about Joseph Vanning?"

"Oh."

"Oh?"

"Yeah, oh."

"What do you think the city pays us for? Don't answer that. We know he was paying the bills for the Robbins girl, and we know he works for your friend White. My bosses have been trying to get something on White for years. So far, all you seem to be doing is stirring things up and making our job harder."

"If you're so smart, how come Ginger is dead?"

"Get the hell out of here before I have you locked up for loitering."

"Friday?"

"What?"

"When this case is over, can I have that slug back for my trophy room?" Hardy didn't wait for an answer but made a very hasty exit.

He grabbed another cab back home and spent the rest of the day reading about Zorba the Greek.

That evening Peg returned his call. They had dinner together and went to the theater. The play was so bad that they left after the first act. He wasn't going to, but in the cab back to her hotel Hardy told Peg what had happened to Ginger. She got very upset. When they got to her room she pleaded a headache and they said good night at her door. Downstairs, it was raining . . .

The night wasn't a total loss. When he got home *Lost Horizon* was on TV.

Chapter Thirteen

The next morning Hardy woke up with a cold. Of course he skipped his workout. Then, after much sneezing and hacking and gargling and aspirin-taking, he called his doctor who said he could come right over.

Dr. Merle Doyle was one of the most beautiful doctors Hardy had ever known. One of the most beautiful women too. She was also strictly business. As far as she was concerned, she was a doctor and Hardy was a patient, even though Hardy pointed out as often as he could that she was a woman and he was a man—a man who was very much attracted to his lovely doctor.

"Shut up, Pat. How can I take your temperature if you insist on talking?"

"I warn you. It's going to be high. What do you expect with you so . . ."

She thrust the thermometer into his mouth and took his wrist. His pulse was going so fast she finally gave up and burst out laughing. "I give up. You're going a mile a minute. I won't even try to take your blood pressure, you'd break the sphygmomanometer. I'd better give you some tranquilizers. If you react to all women this way, you're going to have a heart attack."

He moved in closer and breathed in her scent.

"Not all women . . . just you. That's Replique, isn't it?"

"Keep quiet. Take off your shirt."

"Sure you can take it?"

"Shut up . . . For God's sake, what happened to you?"

Hardy wasn't wearing an undershirt and the bruise on his chest had metamorphosed into a purple monster.

"Pretty, isn't it? Ow . . . that hurts."

She shook her head at him. "Does it ache?" He nodded. She probed him some more, and he winced. "How did it happen?" He told her, and she shook her head again. "Why didn't you come to see me after it happened?"

"I was afraid."

"Of what?"

"You know how I hate doctors' offices. That's one of the reasons I chose you for my doctor . . . so I would have an incentive for coming when I didn't want to."

"Obviously the incentive wasn't enough."

"I brought you my cold, didn't I?"

"Shut up and get dressed. I'll give you some B-12 and something for your cold. Take some aspirin if that bruise aches. Too bad you're allergic to penicillin. Stupid police doctors. The only thing they're good for is to tell you whether somebody's dead or not. Even then they're not always right."

"How would you like to have dinner with me tonight?"

"I'd love to."

"Hey, that's just . . ."

"But you can't make it. You're going to stay home tonight and nurse your cold."

"Very funny. Very funny. Seriously, Merle . . ."

He had lost her attention. She was concentrating on her radio which was playing classical music. She made a face. "Listen to that maniac murder Schumann. He's missing notes left and right. Some pianist! All genius and no technique. Oh . . . good-bye, Pat."

As he came out of Merle Doyle's office, he gave his nose an extra blow. It didn't help. He knew that as soon as he got home he would have to put his mind to the case. He was stumped as it was, and his cold had put him in even less of a mood to work. Avoidance of work was one of Hardy's strongest traits. He decided to walk home.

As he walked, he thought about Peg and how he felt about her. He didn't know. Then he thought about Ruby. He smiled.

There were some antique shops along his route . . . and browsing would delay his getting home. He browsed.

The third shop he went into had a barber chair with a reclining seat . . . where the owner could catch a fast nap whenever he chose to. On an impulse, he bought it.

When the delivery men were gone, Hardy called Holmes out of the bedroom where he had been hiding, and they both admired the barber chair. Hardy thought it looked just fine next to his desk. He thought it felt fine too, as he tested the reclining seat.

109

The chair was on wheels and speeding along a railroad track. Ahead . . . a speeding train was coming toward him. He could see Friday dressed as a Keystone Kop sitting in the engineer's seat. He was shaking his fist. Hardy looked behind. The man without a face was on a handcar chasing him. There was a girl tied to the handcar. Hardy tried to get up, but he was tied to the chair.

The man without a face was now the barber. He came closer, his razor aimed at Hardy's neck. The girl was crying. Hardy was crying. He could hear the train's whistle. His face was wet. Was it tears or was it blood?

Holmes' barking woke him up. As he sat there trying to breathe and trying to shake the dream from his head, he realized the phone was ringing. He picked up the receiver.

"Hello. King Cole?"

It was some stupid woman trying to call the supermarket. Once a month she dialed wrong and got Hardy. He usually hung up on her. This time he took her order. When she was done, he hung up and lit a cigarette. "She'll wait a long time for that food. I hope she's expecting guests. Serves her right."

Holmes barked in agreement, and they both went into the kitchen to get something to eat.

While he and Holmes shared a carrot, Hardy tried to put his thoughts in order, but he couldn't. He remembered seeing a detective in a movie using a bulletin board to organize all his clues and see them at a glance. He didn't have a bulletin board, but since the wall next to his desk was covered in cork, he used it instead and started reviewing. First he pinned up the pictures of Dorothy and Larry Leeds and John

Vanning. Then the program Leeds had given him. Then he put each fact he knew—or thought he knew —on a piece of paper and pinned the paper to the wall.

1. "Dorothy Robbins is dead. She was strangled by a person or persons unknown."

2. "Peg Robbins claims that her sister had been killed by the Organization."

3. "Two people and a dog have been killed in the same building. Also, the victim was mugged six months prior to her death."

4. "Larry Leeds was in love with Dorothy. Larry Leeds is dead."

5. "Joseph Vanning was in love with Dorothy and had been keeping her."

6. "Louis White. Ben Pelligrin. The Organization?"

7. "Joseph Vanning works for Louis White."

8. "Ruby."

9. "Milly."

10. "Ginger."

11. "Ginger was a friend of Dorothy's and she's dead."

The phone rang.

"Hello."

"Tillie Bushman here."

"How are you, Mrs. Bushman?"

"Not so good. How come Amanda Delaney is still walking the streets?"

"I don't know, Mrs. Bushman. Why don't you ask Detective Friday?"

"I'm not asking Friday. I'm asking you. She killed that girl. I know it."

"How do you know it?"

"Before that poor girl died I was in that building

a lot. I caught Amanda sneaking around the halls in a very suspicious manner."

"Where was that?"

"On the fifth floor where Amanda and that girl lived."

"What were you doing there?"

"Spying on Amanda. What else? I told the police about it. But they didn't listen to me."

"I'll call them up, and I'll tell them. They'll listen to me."

"Thanks ever so much. You're a good boy. Bye."

As Hardy dialed Friday's number, he scrawled Tillie Bushman's name and Amanda Delaney's on one of his pieces of paper.

"Hello. Friday speaking."

"This is Pat Hardy."

"Now my day is complete."

" I hate to bother you, but has Tillie Bushman ever told you that she thought Amanda Delaney killed Dorothy Robbins?"

"Lots of times."

"What did you do about it?"

"Look, when Tillie Bushman first started calling, we went and talked to her to see what was up. All we ever ended up writing on the blotter was 'not worth investigating.' She's just a big pain and so are you."

"Sorry about that."

Hardy winced as Friday slammed the phone down in his ear. Then he tore up Tillie Bushman's and Amanda Delaney's pieces of paper and went into the kitchen for some tapioca and ice cream.

Afterward he stared at the cork wall, debating whether or not to forget it and look for a movie on television. He surprised himself and voted against the movie.

He thought about Vivica Johnson's visit. He indulged himself with a few moments of sex fantasy and then wrote some more.

12. "Why did White find it necessary to send Vivica Johnson with that elaborate warning and bribe?"

13. "Is Amanda Delaney just a kook and a whisky thief?"

He went back to paper number eight, the one with Ruby's name, and added: "Whose side is she on?"

14. "Why is Friday trying to get me to drop the case? Is it because I get in his hair, or are there other reasons?"

Typically paranoid, he wondered if perhaps Steve wasn't involved in some way.

15. "What about Steve? Is it just a coincidence that Ginger and Ruby were at his place and that Ginger was killed there?"

16. "Am I in love with Peg?"

He tore up number sixteen and reached for the phone. He changed his mind. He had been going to call Peg. Instead he considered what he had written about Peg and tried to breathe. Neither activity seemed to do any good. He went into the bathroom to get a decongestant. En route he decided that, for his own protection, he wouldn't call Peg. Not for a while. At least not while he was getting these erratic thoughts.

He had never considered being in love before. It had never occurred to him. He loved himself too much. While he was busy being in love with himself he admired himself in a full-length mirror. He didn't look too admirable.

"Hello, fats."

His pants were pulling just a little bit at the waist. Too much laziness and not enough exercise. He stripped down to his skin.

"Ech. Cold or no cold, today we work." Hardy changed into his sweat clothes and went into the gym.

He finished off with thirty minutes on the mounted track bike. After that concession to aerobics he took his shower. He felt pretty good too, and, pleasant surprise, he was breathing through his nose.

Hardy felt so good he went back to his desk and prepared to make some phone calls. Wearing a towel, he sat down and dialed Ruby's number, not really knowing if he was calling her in order to work or because he was horny.

Ruby's answering service picked up. She was in Chicago on a booking and would be out of town for a week. Frustrated, Hardy took the program from the wall and started looking up phone numbers in the casting guide. He had just finished his list when the doorbell rang. Cautiously, he looked out the window. It was Peg. Immediately he got aroused. He was in a rut. Quickly, and much against his judgment, he threw on a pair of pants. Then he and Holmes went to the door and let Peg in.

"Hi. Take these." She handed him a couple of packages and took off her sunglasses. "I waited for you to call me all morning. Well, if the mountain won't come to Mohammed, Mohammed just has to . . . What happened to your chest?"

Remembering how upset she had gotten when he had told her about Ginger's death, Hardy didn't go into details. "I got it crime fighting."

She pecked him on the mouth and said, "My poor

114

detective." She grabbed his hand. "Why didn't you call me?"

"Ow," said Hardy, as he pulled his hand away. She noticed a big welt on his hand.

"Oh, you poor thing. You're wounded everywhere. Did you get that crime fighting too?"

"No. I burned it when I was cooking."

Peg collapsed on the couch, laughing. Hardy saw how funny it was and joined her. Each time one of them stopped laughing, they would look at each other and start again. Of course, Holmes joined them in the noise-making. Hardy was the first to stop.

"All right. That's enough. It wasn't that funny. Holmes, shut up!"

"Yes, it was," said Peg through her giggles.

She looked so pretty and appealing as she sat there laughing, Hardy kissed her. He didn't need a reason. He was definitely falling in love with her.

"Mmm," said Peg after a moment. "That's the best laugh stopper I ever heard of."

"How about some more?"

"Why not? Oh my gosh, the ice cream."

"The what?"

"Ice cream. I brought you a present."

"To hell with the ice cream."

"Oh, behave yourself. You're a wounded man. Ice cream's the best thing for you. It'll cool you off."

"Just what I need. What's in the other package?"

"Another present. Open it. When did you get that?" she asked, pointing to the barber chair.

"Today," said Hardy, as he opened the package. "Hey, that's great." It was a doormat with the inscription "go away" on it.

She inspected his bulletin wall and answered him. "I thought you'd like it. It suits your personality."

Hardy ignored that and put the mat out in the hall. When he came back in, he found Peg in the kitchen. "Hi," she said. "I hope you like vanilla."

"My favorite kind." He crossed over and kissed her on the back of the neck. "Do you know what I've been thinking?"

"Yes, and the answer is no. My daddy told me to be careful of men like you." She finished loading up Hardy's plate and licked the spoon. "Why don't you forget about working today and take me somewhere?"

"Because the lady I work for pays me a lot of good money, and she's not getting much return on it as it is. I've been thinking about that, Peg. This could go on forever and at two hundred a day . . ."

"No," Peg said, "I don't want you to stop, if that's what you mean. But it's nice to know I've gotten to you."

"What do you mean by that?"

"When a private detective named Patrick Hardy starts worrying about a girl, and that the two hundred dollars a day that he's getting is too much, she's gotten to him."

They both looked very uncomfortable, and then Hardy lit a cigarette. "How about a little music?"

She nodded, and he went to the record changer. "Wait till you hear this," he said. "Stan Getz. You like my new chair?"

She grinned and nodded and they sat and listened to the music and said very little to each other. After about ten minutes some kids went by the window and Holmes started barking at them. The mood was broken.

"Seriously, Peg, I think . . ."

"You sound like a comic that just bombed. 'Seriously, folks.' Why don't you stop being so serious and take me somewhere?"

"It's a deal. Tonight we'll do the town. I'll take you to a couple of clubs and . . ."

"No, I don't mean that. I hate clubs and bars and things like that. I mean now. Let's go to the zoo or to a museum or just walk in Central Park."

"O.K. But as of today, I'm off salary."

"All right, but I still want you on the case. So I'll take care of your expenses and, as an incentive, if you find whoever killed Dot, I'll pay you ten thousand dollars."

"But . . ."

"Don't worry about it, darling. I can afford it."

"All right. Now that that sordid stuff is taken care of, I'm going to take you out and sweep you off your feet. I'm going to show you all the exciting and hidden wonders of New York. Let's go."

Where are we going?"

"The Frick Museum."

So they went to the Frick and the Guggenheim and the children's zoo in Central Park. They acted like people in love, but they didn't make love. Peg said she wanted to be sure. And much to Hardy's astonishment, he didn't mind—too much.

They spent the weekend that way, enjoying each other and forgetting about murders and detection. They were together. They talked. They did things people in love do, and each night he took her back to her hotel. On Friday they watched "The French Chef" and both learned how to make poires au gratin. On Saturday they ate Chinese food. (Hardy taught her his incorrect but effective method of using chopsticks.) That night they stayed in and watched "The

117

Late Show." And on Sunday they did the *Times'*
crossword puzzle, commiserated with Mary Worth,
made faces at the politicians who lied to them through
the magic of television, and he took her back to her
hotel.

Chapter Fourteen

Monday morning. His cold was gone. But playtime was over. After an enjoyable workout he called Peg . . . just to say good morning. After twenty minutes of saying good morning, they said good-bye . . . for another five minutes. Then breakfast.

He turned the TV on for company and started calling the people on the list he had compiled on Thursday.

It was all wasted effort. After Dorothy and Larry Leeds had met, they stayed aloof from the rest of the company.

Hardy called the producer of the play. No luck there. He barely remembered who Dorothy Robbins was. "There are so many of them every year. It's hard to keep track."

She had gotten the job on her own so there was no agent for Hardy to call.

His attention was drawn to the TV. Wasn't that a familiar face? It was Macker on a beer commercial.

Grateful for an excuse to break the monotony, Hardy dialed Macker's number.

"Hello."

"Hi, Steve. Pat."

"Oh, it's you."

"Wow, your telephone personality is great today. Hey, I just spotted your commercial."

"Tell me about it another time, will you? I'm in the sack."

"Alone?"

"God! Pat, sometimes you ask the dumbest questions."

Slightly deflated, Hardy hung up the telephone. Moodily, he went into the kitchen. In an effort to soothe his bruised sensitivities, he made himself a salami sandwich on white bread with ketchup and a cup of tea. He felt a lot better.

Hardy stared at the papers on the bulletin wall and made out a new one. In large print he wrote: "MO-TIVE—MEANS—OPPORTUNITY." Tired out from all his labors, he looked among his books for something he had read before. Just the thing. *Fer-De-Lance* by Rex Stout. He smiled and settled down in his barber chair for a visit with an old friend.

He had gotten sleepy and soon he was counting nude and semi-nude girls leaping over racing hurdles, their breasts billowing in the wind. He could make out some of their faces. Ruby, Peg, Milly, Ginger. Even Amanda Delaney, her ponderous teats swinging with the rest of them.

Ginger was falling and the others were ignoring her plight and trampling her.

Ginger became Dorothy Robbins, or was it . . . ? Then she became Larry Leeds, who in turn became

Patrick Hardy. The trampling feet wouldn't stop. They pounded at his arms, his chest and his face.

Through it all Hardy could see the man without a face watching him. He tried to scream, and then decided he didn't want to. The trampling feet had become breasts. The breasts reached out and comforted him, soothing his arms and chest and face.

He saw himself: a balloon, ready to burst. He was full to overflowing. The pressure increased—fuller and fuller and fuller.

Release. All doors opened, and pent-up energy escaped. Ears popped, sinuses cleared, cavities emptied. He was all sticky. Blood. He was covered with blood. He forced himself awake.

After the initial shock of the dream was over, Hardy smiled at himself. He shook his head and went into the bathroom, muttering, "I wonder what Freud would say about that."

In the shower it came to him that he had never checked out Dorothy Robbins' agent, the one who booked her exotic act. Now how could he find out who the agent was? He buttoned the bath kilt around himself and went back to his desk and dialed information. They gave him the number of AGVA, who in turn gave him the name of the agent, Ernie Turner.

"How's that for a shrewd piece of detection, Holmes old boy? Instantaneous results. That's me, Patrick Hardy, Instant Detective."

He dialed information again and got Ernie Turner's address. Fortified with that and a ham omelette he went downtown.

Times Square was its usual self. A policeman directed the auto traffic while all the other traffic went on around him. It was a block for sad and lonely people. Hardy's mind took off on a philosophical stream.

121

"Can't find a job? Just get fired? Goofing off? Go to Times Square and watch the fairies. Let one pick you up. Later you can beat the hell out of him and take his money. Not your style? Go to a horny movie and watch some nude women beat each other up. If that doesn't move you, there's always a pimp around or a man who can get you a couple of sticks or even something a little stronger. Don't forget the bookstores with all those great pictures of either sex. Or you can eat burnt frankfurters and enjoy the atmosphere of sweat and fried onions and wine and stale piss. Later you can go to the dance parlor and try to connect there or flash some money in front of the shoe store. If someone doesn't crack your head and steal it from you one of the many hookers who work the area is sure to notice you. You can get most anything you want in the Times Square area. Just don't jump that light where the traffic cop is. He's there to enforce the law and he'd have to give you a ticket."

Hardy plowed through the crowd and the stench of sweat and fried onions and crammed down a couple of burnt frankfurters. Then he went back into one of the bookstores he had thought about and looked through several books he had no intention of buying.

He was aroused. Self-consciously, he put down the last book, resolved to get himself a woman for that night to alleviate his condition, mentally put down all the other men in the store for being there, put his newspaper over the front of his pants and left.

As he waited for the light, his gaze took in the weird assortment of misfits congregating around Father Duffy's statue. So dirty and cruddy even hippies wouldn't want them. Hardy wondered why he ever left his apartment.

122

The light still said Don't Walk, but he jaywalked across and went into Ernie Turner's building. A short, fat man with a smelly Italian cigar in his face was methodically emptying the only desk in the small office. Some papers flew in and around the wastebasket, others into the imitation leather briefcase.

Hardy cleared his throat. "I hope I'm not interrupting."

Short and fat looked up. "What do you want? We're closed."

"I'm looking for Ernie Turner."

"That's me. What do you want?"

"Going somewhere?"

"Yeah, Miami. I'm retiring."

"Why?"

"Who wants to know? Never mind, I don't care. None of your business. Now get out of here."

"I think I'll stay for a while. Mr. Turner, my name is Pat Hardy and I'm inves . . ."

"Suit yourself. I'm leaving. I got a plane to catch." He took a fast last look around, glared at Hardy and left.

Nonplused, Hardy sat down and tried to figure out his next move. Expecting nothing, he searched the office. He wasn't disappointed. He found nothing.

After a lunch of veal and peppers he meandered around, trying not to let his mind focus on anything. He walked uptown, then east, then uptown some more, just smoking and looking at girls. At 53rd Street he went into the little park and ordered Sanka. Then he smoked some more and stared at the waterfall.

A car backfiring snapped Hardy out of his reverie. He admonished himself for goofing off and went home.

After saying hello to Holmes he made himself a peanut butter and jelly sandwich and prepared to go to work. As he took a bite of the sandwich, the phone rang. He lifted the receiver, but before he could speak, the voice at the other end spoke. "Hello, Mr. Hardy. Why don't you go out and start up your car? You'll get a big bang out of it."

Hardy hung up the phone. The food in his mouth turned sour. He went to the bathroom and rinsed his mouth and drank a lot of water. Then he relieved himself and lit a cigarette. His knee ached. He chewed a couple of nails and stared into space. He turned the TV on and off again, opened the refrigerator door, took nothing out, lit another cigarette and went to the bathroom again. Then he sat at his desk and examined the grain of the wood in the floor. No use, no matter what he did, the car was still out there. He decided to call the police. But what if there were no bomb and the caller wanted him to call the police on a false alarm. If that caller caused him to do that often enough, the police would never listen to him and he would no longer be a threat. "Ha . . . some threat." That might not be a bad idea. It might be the best way out of the mess once and for all. No, that wouldn't work. He went to the door. Holmes started barking.

"Shut up, Holmes. Shut up. Go to bed."

Holmes went, snarling under his breath, trying to figure out why he was being punished when he hadn't done anything. Hardy went out to his VW parked in the bus stop and stared at it. There was no ticket on the windshield.

"Gee, am I lucky!"

Gingerly, he opened the engine compartment. A piece of wood was tied to the ignition wire with some pink ribbon. Across the wood someone had inked in the word "dynamite." Also tied to the ribbon was a card which read, "Sorry we couldn't get you the real stuff. Maybe next time."

Very slowly, Hardy undid the ribbon and removed the ersatz dynamite. He closed up the car and went back into his apartment. The phone was ringing and Holmes was barking. Hardy ignored both and wished the service would hurry up and answer the phone. They didn't. It was a losing battle. Hardy pounced on the phone and answered it.

"Hello."

"Hi, Pat. It's me—Peg."

"Yeah, Peg. What do you want?"

"Well, I like that."

"Look, Peg, is it all right if I . . ."

Before Hardy could finish what he was saying another voice joined in from Peg's end. "Let me talk to him. Hello, hello. Who's this?"

"This is Pat Hardy. Who's this? Peg? Are you all right?"

"Don't worry. This is Reverend Francis X. Robbins. I understand my daughter has paid you good money to do a job. Why haven't you done it?"

Hardy then heard a series of mutterings, male and female. Then Peg came back on. "Pat? I'm sorry. That was my father."

"So I gathered."

"I'm just as surprised as you are. I went out for some lunch, and when I came back he was here waiting for me. He wants to . . ."

"I'll tell you what I want." It was Reverend Robbins again. "I want to straighten out this mess and get out of this city for good, and take my daughter with me. What? Peg wants to talk to you some more."

"I'm sorry, Pat. May we come over to see you?"

"Sure. Come ahead."

"In about a half hour?"

"See you then."

He turned on the TV and sat down. With Charlie Chan for company he waited for Peg and her father.

The doorbell rang as Charlie was wrapping his case up. Hardy wished life could be as easy as he went to the door.

Reverend Francis X. Robbins was a surprise. Hardy expected a cliché minister from the Bible Belt. Instead, he was a smooth-looking old gentleman who made an off-the-rack suit look custom-made. He took a drink, but frowned when Hardy offered one to Peg.

"All right," he said. "Tell me about it."

Hardy sighed and started to bring the reverend up to date. Suddenly, for no reason, the old man interrupted and started talking about Dorothy. "She's a great girl. Wait till you meet her. Smart as a whip that girl of mine. You know what they say: daddy's little girl. Why didn't you call me and tell me what happened, Peg? At least I could have been here for the funeral. I swear, Peg, more and more everyday you get more like Dottie. I don't know what I'm going to do with you."

Just as suddenly he switched gears. "All right, young fellow. I've heard enough. You seem to be handling it right. You finish it up, you hear, and be quick about it. You catch Dot's killer." Then he started crying and stopped almost immediately. "None of that now. You find him. That's what you've got to do. Peg and I are going back home. That's what we've got to do."

Peg reached for her father's hand. "No, Papa. You go home. I have to stay here and help Mr. Hardy."

He regained some composure and chuckled. "What can you do? You're just a babe in the woods."

"I'm staying."

Hardy was embarrassed at being in the middle of their emotions. "Peg, maybe your father's right. Maybe you should go back home."

She shook her head. "Not you too. I'm staying."

"All right," said Hardy. "Why don't you go home with your father and then come back in a couple of weeks?"

What are you trying to pull?" said Reverend Robbins. "You think I need a nursemaid or something. I came here by myself, I can go back by myself. Peg can stay if she wants to. She's got nerve. Glad somebody in the family still has. Getting to be more like Dot everyday. You should have called me, Peg. I should have been here." He drained his drink. "Well, nice talking to you, Mr. Hardy. Sorry to rush off like this, but if I'm going to catch a plane out of here tonight, I had better get at it."

As they left, Peg let him know that she would call later.

Hardy tried to comprehend the Lewis Carroll scene he had just watched. He decided it wasn't worth it and found refuge in a drink.

As he sat there Holmes shoved a mangled rawhide ball at him. Hardy made a halfhearted attempt to take it away from him. Holmes growled hopefully in playful anger.

"Not now, Holmes."

Holmes insisted. Hardy made another grab and now the tug of war was on in earnest. Hardy won but fell on his ass with the effort. Holmes was on him growling and licking his face. Hardy laughed. They wrestled a little more until Holmes grew bored and crawled in a corner and went to sleep. Hardy poured himself another drink and started thumbing through his *TV Guide*. The phone rang.

"Hi, stud. How are you?" It was Ruby.

"Hi, Red. Good to hear your voice."

"If that's your thing I'll send you a recording."

"I want a little more than that from you."

"Really? What do you mean by that?"

"If I told you, you wouldn't be able to stand it. Are you back in town?"

"No, I'm in Chicago. From here I go to Detroit, then I'll be back in New York."

"When's then?"

"About a week or so."

He lit a cigarette. "Do we have a date?"

He could sense her smile over the phone. "Your place or mine?"

"Well," he said, "if you're going to argue, forget it."

"Who's arguing? I'm horny already. I'll call you when I get in. So long, lover."

"Hey! What am I supposed to do until then?"

"Sublimate. Oh, by the by, you might be interested in knowing that Milly is working at the Variety Theatre in L.A."

"Thanks, Red. See you in about a week."

She hissed at him by drawing her breath in quickly and audibly in what was meant to be a provocative sound. "If I can wait that long."

He hung up the phone, relit a new cigarette from the old one and stared into space and sublimated.

After L.A. information had given him the number, Hardy dialed the Variety Theatre. Milly wasn't there yet. Rather than leave word with the doorman he decided to call back later.

He put on some old Glenn Miller records and made another attempt at reading *Giles Goat-Boy*. After ten minutes he gave up on the book and simply listened to the music.

Holmes heard the motorcycle before Hardy did. They both got up and watched Steve Macker come to the door. Hardy told Holmes to shut up and let Macker in.

"Hi," said Hardy. "I was just about to have a drink. You want? I found this great almond wine, it's called Sicilian Gold. You want some?"

Macker put down his helmet and laughed. "What a coincidence." He pulled out a repacked Marlboro. "I'll stick to Acapulco Gold."

Hardy frowned. "I thought you gave up on that stuff."

"Relax. A little grass never hurt anyone. Don't get moral on me."

"Not moral, just chicken. I have enough trouble without you turning on in my apartment. With my luck some cop with an educated nose would come walking by, and whap."

"All right. You want to take a ride? You have my other helmet."

"You mean with you high?"

Macker snorted. "Will you relax? I always get high when I drive. How else could I stand the traffic?"

"Why not? Hey, I'm sorry about calling before."

"Forget it. How could you know? Besides, she was a lousy lay. Hey, maybe we'll shoot some pool. And if you're looking for some action, there's going to be a poker game at my place tonight."

It was a great time for Hardy. When he got back to his apartment later and tallied up he found he had lost twelve dollars playing pool and thirty-six dollars playing poker.

He turned on the final minutes of Johnny Carson and dialed the Variety Theatre again.

"Wait a minute. She's right here. Hey, Milly. It's for you."

"Hello."

"Hello, Milly. Pat Hardy. Remember me?"

Milly didn't answer.

"Hey," said Hardy. "Don't hang up on me."

"I remember you. What do you want?"

"I thought you might like to talk to me."

"Big joke. Ginger talked to you and look where it got her. Do me a favor, will you? Forget I exist."

"Look, I'm sorry about Ginger, but I'm also sorry about Dorothy Robbins. If you'll just answer . . ."

She was working hard to hold back her tears. "Mister, please, please leave me alone. I don't know anything. Please leave me alone. I just want to be left alone."

She didn't bother to hang up the phone. As she walked away, Hardy could hear the receiver bouncing against the wall. Hardy hung up and went to bed.

Chapter Fifteen

Tuesday looked like it was going to be a good day. And he hadn't dreamed. He had a good workout and a better breakfast.

"Come on, Holmes. Let's go get the mail."

As they went out, Holmes barked at the world to let it know he was around. Some children were playing in front of the building. He barked at them too. A tiny Yorkshire on its way out barked back at Holmes, and Holmes hid behind Hardy. Hardy smiled ruefully.

"You're my dog, all right."

There was no mail for him and none for Dorothy Robbins either. Holmes was tugging at his leash so Hardy let himself be dragged toward the park. On the way Holmes sniffed at everything.

"Get away from there. This whole town is starting to smell like one big dog turd."

Hardy stood at the corner and smiled at the cute blonde waiting to cross. Holmes got very interested in her female poodle. The light turned green, and the girl started to cross. Hardy stopped her.

"Be careful. Most people jump this light."

She smiled back at him and crossed anyway, nearly getting hit by a car that did jump the light. She turned and smiled again and went on her way. Holmes, in a state of excitement, pulled at his leash in an effort to chase after her. Hardy noticed the dog's erection and shook his head.

"Sorry, pal. I guess they're not interested." He chuckled, "That's my dog." He unleashed Holmes and they went into the park where the animal first watered the grass and then tried to eat it. Hardy constantly nagged at the dog.

"Don't eat grass. Get away from the pigeons, you'll get brain fever."

They went down to the boat basin where Hardy bought an ice cream. That's when the two heavyweights jumped him. He crammed the ice cream into one set of eyes and whipped at the other with the dog leash. While ice cream face was busy wiping, Hardy took one clip on the head from the other and repaid it with several chops to the body. He turned back to the first one, who had Holmes to contend with. The dog was on top of him, snarling and biting. The two attackers didn't like the way things were going and off they went. Hardy started to chase them. That's when his knee tricked out.

As he sat there catching his breath and pushing his knee back in place, Hardy watched the crop of humanity in the park. Their main aim in life seemed to be to avoid his look and ignore what had happened. The only one who got involved was Holmes, who was busy licking him and shaking with fright. As they sat on the ground, Hardy petted the poodle and tried to calm him.

"You really are my dog, aren't you? An out-and-out coward . . . just like me. Do you know I love you? Truth. I love you because I feel for you. You're my dog. You're me, and that's love. Two grade A cowards. But, we manage to deal with it, don't we? In a world that glorifies heroes, we cope, and we get along." Holmes wagged his tail and shook some more.

Hardy caught his breath and looked around. He had enough trouble without having someone hearing this conversation and thinking him a nut. As an afterthought he decided he didn't care what they thought. "Screw 'em."

The two "heroes" limped toward home, grateful for each other. On the way a cop gave Hardy a ticket for having his dog off the leash.

Laura opened the door for him. "Mr. Hardy, what on earth happened to your face?"

"I think I poked into somebody else's business."

"If that's supposed to be a hint, I'm not going to take it. Sit down and I'll fix it for you."

"What are you going to do?"

"I'm going to press a knife on that lump and get the swelling down."

"Oh no, you're not."

"Oh, Mr. Hardy, you're such a big baby."

"You bet I am."

"O.K., you can relax. I'll use some ice cubes to take the swelling down . . . but the knife would be better."

Later, while he was dressing, Hardy kept looking at his face in the bedroom mirror. He was dressing in order to go downtown and have it out with White. He was very angry; he was also very scared. He could hear Laura in the next room watching her soap opera.

She was warning the heroine not to listen to the lies of the smooth-talking villain.

"That's not true. Don't you listen to him. Dear God, if you believe that, you'll believe anything. He is too the father of that girl's baby. Don't you listen to him."

Hardy filled his pockets with the necessaries and left the bedroom and the apartment. Holmes gave him one feeble yap, and Laura didn't even notice.

Absent-mindedly, Hardy got into his bug and turned on the ignition. He nearly had a coronary when the noise of the engine turning over reminded him of what had happened yesterday. After he recovered, he drove to the garage, put the car away and took a cab downtown.

As he rode downtown he thought out what he would say to White. The top of his brain dealt with the protests and accusations he would make, but deep down he knew he was going there to tell White he had won. He was going to quit.

Hardy wouldn't let himself think of what would happen between him and Peg when she found out. He had simply had enough. He wanted to go back to following wives for husbands and husbands for wives . . . and if Peg hated him for it, at least he would have his comfort and his piece of mind—and his life.

The cab was headed for Rockefeller Center, but Hardy paid the driver at Columbus Circle and started to walk. He passed the Jelly Apple Shop. The sweet smell somehow made him think of death. The jelly smells mixed with cheap power and perfume that pervaded the block.

The hookers were out early today, and in force. A lot of good-looking young hookers who would

134

grow up to be ugly-looking old hookers. It was probably their busy season. Hardy took them in as he walked. They were a varied group. Slutty types, chic mod types, and there was one straight out of Peck & Peck . . . or maybe she was just lost. None of the older stuff though. Hardy guessed that they preferred bars and their own apartments. He grinned as he dubbed the street "The Prostie Prep School." It crossed his mind that not one of them had ever propositioned him. He was secretly pleased that he didn't look like a mark. But before the thought left him, one of the younger ladies slid up to him and made her pitch.

"Hey, Mister, you want to go on a date?"

Hardy frowned, then smiled and shook his head. A tiny portion of ego had been deflated. Past the record stores now, with their mixed bag of sounds. He stopped to look at the nude album covers. Hardy wondered if there were any records inside. His thoughts then switched to Ruby, then to Peg. How was he going to tell Peg? More to the point, he'd better hurry and tell White and get it over with.

Rockefeller Center was teeming with tourists. At least it wasn't Wednesday. Matinee day was no day for a native New Yorker to be midtown.

The soothing music in the elevator did not soothe his nervous stomach.

The same bosomy receptionist told him that Mr. White would see him in a moment. While he waited, he stared at her chest and smoked a cigarette.

"You can go in now."

"Huh?"

She arched her back a little and said it again. "You can go in now."

"Come in, Mr. Hardy, but don't sit down." Louis

135

White had lost the pleasant manner he had shown to Hardy the last time.

Hardy started to speak, but White interrupted him. "You did not come here to talk. You came to listen. Up until now I ignored you. I let others handle your case and toy with you as they would. I warned you not to interfere in my affairs. You chose to ignore me and involve yourself. You see too many people and make too many phone calls. From now on you are not just a nuisance, you are an enemy. I like to know what my enemies are doing. From now on you shall be watched until the day you die . . . and if you are not very careful that may be very soon. Get out!"

"But I came to tell you that I'm quitting the case. I'm through. I'm out."

"That may be the truth, and then again it may be a ploy. Nevertheless, it is too late. You have involved yourself. You are involved."

Hardy looked about the room as if hoping to find the answer to his problem there. Ben Pelligrin stood in a corner, smirking at him. White spoke again. "Take a good look at Mr. Pelligrin. From time to time he shall be keeping tabs on you. Don't be surprised if you look over your shoulder and see him there. You should have kept the money and taken a long trip. Good-bye, Mr. Hardy."

Ben Pelligrin opened the door and pointed Hardy out. As he wandered in a daze into the waiting room he could still hear White talking to Ben Pelligrin. "God, how I hate amateurs."

Hardy didn't remember going home, but there he was. As he emptied his pockets he noticed there was a little dust on the corner of his clothes valet. He absent-mindedly cursed Laura for doing a sloppy job and resolved to fire her. He fried himself some liver, had two stiff drinks and prepared to go to bed. The phone rang.

"Hello."

"Hello, Darling. It's me, Peg."

"Hi, Honey. Look, if you don't mind I don't feel like talking now. Let's talk tomorrow, huh?"

"What's wrong? Is it because of what happened yesterday with my father?"

"No, nothing like that. I just don't feel like talking, that's all."

"All right," she pouted, "if that's the way . . . Pat! Do you have a woman with you?"

"Goddamn it, no! I just don't feel like talking to anyone. Good night."

He turned out the light and called Holmes up on the bed for company and solace and tried to go to sleep.

He was on a medieval torture rack. The machinery was pulling at his arms and legs. His knee ached. His arms hurt. He cried out, but no sound came. The full cast of characters was around the rack, all dressed in Borgia clothing.

Louis White was the master torturer. He kept telling the man without a face to turn the rack again. Peg and Ruby were clawing at Hardy's groin. Macker and Friday and Reverend Robbins stood by and watched. Amanda Delaney appeared with a cat in her arms and threw the animal at his eyes. He turned his face and saw Ruby doing her strip number, but this time she was using a skull instead of a swan. Ginger and Milly were dancing behind her as a chorus. The only problem was that Ginger was dead and Milly was dragging her through her paces. Vanning was applauding and yelling, "Take it off." Mrs. Bushman was conferring with Dr. Merle Doyle, and after

137

much head-nodding, Mrs. Bushman brought over some chicken soup. Hardy couldn't eat it, so she gave it to Holmes who was cowering under the rack.

White motioned to the man without a face. As he came closer the face took form. It was Macker . . . No, it was Friday . . . No, it was Reverend Robbins. The reverend started praying over him, then the face changed again . . . it was Larry Leeds and he had a pair of scissors sticking out of him. Vivica Johnson appeared and took the scissors and started writing on Hardy's body. Laura materialized and took the scissors which changed into a knife. She was almost on him. The man without a face shook his head and took the knife away from her. The knife became a gun. The man without a face said: "Tough luck, Fatso," and shot Hardy in the stomach. He screamed. "Oh my God! Oh God, please don't let me die! I don't want to get hurt. Oh God, please don't let me die!"

He felt his heart stop and his lungs fill with poison. Gasping, he forced himself awake and ran to the bathroom, spitting up phlegm and fear. When he was able to breathe again he gargled with mouthwash to get the taste of death out of his mouth and drank a lot of water. For some weird reason he couldn't get the smell of jelly apples out of his mind. It made him feel sick. He sat down and tried to think of nothing at all.

His left arm hurt. It hurt a great deal. As he went back to the bathroom to get the liniment he flicked on the TV. The liniment didn't seem to do any good, and the TV wasn't working.

"Not my week, Holmes. Definitely not my week." He fiddled with the TV for a while, trying to ignore the pain. The TV wouldn't start working, and the arm wouldn't stop hurting.

"Shit . . . shit . . . shit!"

He lit a cigarette and called Dr. Merle Doyle. She told him to come right over.

In spite of the pain in his arm, he lugged the TV with him to drop off at the shop.

Merle Doyle was very solicitous, but the pain didn't go away. She poked the back of his hand with a pin, took X-rays and, much to Hardy's disgust, took some blood samples.

"It's probably just a sprain," she said. "It'll probably go away in a few weeks. I'll let you know if anything shows up in the tests."

She checked the bruise on his head. "The outside of your head will get better . . . inside I doubt. Let me look at your knee. Bend it. Good. Don't worry. I won't have to aspirate it. Pat, you really should consider an operation. I'm sure that meniscus is tearing more and more every time you traumatize the knee."

"Thank you, but no thank you. You put those knives back where they belong. I hate to do you out of a split fee from your favorite butcher, but . . . forget it."

"All right. How does your chest feel?"

Hardy conformed to type and leered at her. "I've often wondered that about you."

"Oh, you're incorrigible. Get out. I have some people out there who really need me. Don't say it. Don't say you need me. It's too early in the day."

"O.K. You win. I'm leaving."

"Soak the knee in a hot tub and do those exercises I showed you. You are a mess."

"Yes, ma'am. What do I do about this damn ache in my arm?"

"Take some aspirin."

"Gee, I feel like I'm back in the army."

Her attention was back to her radio. Liszt this time. He sneaked a quick buss on her cheek and left.

When he got home he picked up the mail and fed Holmes. Then he looked at the mail. Junk for him and one letter for Dorothy Robbins. It looked like a bill. Hardy put it down and went to get the aspirin he needed. Then he went to turn on the TV, but it wasn't there. He turned on the radio and stared at the cork wall. Thinking about the pain in his arm and his predicament and how cruel life was to him, he picked up the envelope and opened it. It was a bill . . . for a safety deposit box.

He put a cigarette in his mouth and didn't light it. He chewed the filter and scratched Holmes behind the ear and listened to the music. "What do you put in a safety deposit box?" Holmes tried to get in his lap. Hardy shooed him away and tossed the soggy cigarette in the ashtray. He couldn't find any others so he retrieved the old one and lit it. "What," and he scratched the match, "do you put in a safety deposit box?" He threw the bill in the wastebasket and pretended he was interested in creating smoke rings. When he finished the cigarette, he searched out a fresh pack and smoked some more. Three cigarettes later, he fished the bill out and called Peg.

"Peg, was there a safety deposit box key in your sister's effects?"

There was a pause, then she sort of laughed. "No, I don't think so." Her voice went up a note. "Why?"

"Too bad. A bill just came today for a box. What's in it may be important. Do you think you could pretend to be Dot? Can you do her signature?"

She paused again. "I suppose I can."

"O.K. We could do it legally, but I don't want to

140

wait. What we have to do is pretend you're Dot. We pay the bill, then go down to the vault and . . . uh, you say you lost both keys and you pay them to bust into the box. I think it costs something like twenty-five bucks. Meet me at the bank . . . No. We still have time. Come up here, and we'll run through what we have to do."

"Pat . . . do you . . . ?"

"Hey, in case you haven't noticed, I think I'm in love with you." He hung up quickly and sweated a little.

He took a quick shower and shaved while he waited for Peg. While he was combing his hair for the third time, she rang the bell.

Inside, she took off her sunglasses and came up to him. "Hmm," she said. "You smell nice. Tell me again."

"What?"

"Come on, you jerk. Tell me again."

"Well, first we go to the bank . . ."

"Stop being an idiot and tell me you love me."

"I love you."

"Again."

"I love you. I love you. I love you."

"That's nice." They kissed. Their tongues searched each other out and made love. When they came up for air, Hardy's legs were shaking. She teased him with her eyes a bit and then said, "We'll file that under unfinished business. Right now I have a surprise for you." She reached into her purse and with a burlesque of a magician's gesture she brought her hand back out and opened it. "*Voilà!*"

"Peg . . . Is that the key? You found it."

"Give that gentleman ten silver dollars and an opportunity to go for the big prize—me."

141

"Peg, you're fabulous. If you could cook, I'd marry you."

"Careful."

"Hm? Oh, yeah. Was there a little envelope . . . that the key came in?"

"Yes. Here it is."

"Good. That gives the number of the box."

Peg checked her face in her compact and fixed her lips. "Where's the bank?"

Hardy smiled sourly. "Rockefeller Center."

"What's the joke?"

"I'll tell you sometime. Let's run this through a couple of times." They rehearsed what Peg was going to do for a while, till Peg said, "That's enough. I'm as ready as I'll ever be. Do you have any beer?"

They shared a can of beer and a cigarette and went out. Peg scanned the street. "Where's your car?"

"We'll take a cab." They walked over to West End and found a taxi immediately. He wasn't sure, but he thought a face he had seen near his apartment had gotten into a cab just behind them. When they passed the Lincoln Towers, Hardy checked again. The cab was still behind them. He tried to forget about it. They were traveling a very logical route downtown.

At 59th Street the other cab was still with them. Hardy put some bills in the money tray, grabbed Peg's hand and bolted out into the traffic. Brake screeches and curses followed them as they drove down into the subway. While Peg tried to catch her breath, Hardy thought.

"Come on," he said. "This way."

"Would you mind telling me what's going on?"

"I'm not sure, but I think we're being followed. I'd rather be safe than sorry."

"But who'd be following us?"

"Who do you think? The Organization."

He regrabbed her hand and walked her to another flight of stairs. They came up next to Central Park. Hardy took a quick look around and then scooted into the park and started east. Peg nervously kept looking behind them. "Pat, do you want to forget the whole thing?"

"Yes, I do. But it's too late for that. Stop looking around like that, it makes you easier to spot." Silently they hurried to Fifth Avenue, left the park and started downtown. The streets were crowded. The matinee mob was out in full force. They overshot their destination and cut through the channel, past the ice rink, up the stairs and across the street, into the building where the bank was. The same building, much to Hardy's regret, where Louis White had his office.

Peg paid the bill and Hardy paced and watched. While they waited for the elevator to the vault he looked up and saw Ben Pelligrin entering the bank. Pelligrin didn't seem to see them. Hardy crowded around Peg and jabbed impatiently at the button.

"What's wrong?" said Peg.

"Ben Pelligrin, one of the Organization's top men. He's here."

Peg made a sharp noise in her throat. She looked around and zeroed in on the enemy. She seemed to shrink a little and she too started jabbing at the button. When the car arrived they tried to enter without giving thought to the people leaving. Ben Pelligrin, who had no idea that they were in the bank, looked up at the commotion and caught Hardy's frightened face as the door was closing. Hardy tried to control the claustrophobia the small car brought on. The

143

essence of matron's face powder and stale cigar didn't help.

In the vault, it was easy. Peg showed the key in the envelope. The guard gave her a slip to fill out and looked up the file card. He gave a perfunctory look at her signature and went in to open the box.

Hardy cleared his throat. "Do you have a room?" The guard nodded. He led them into a room, placed the box on a table and left them alone. They traded tight smiles, and Hardy motioned with his head for Peg to go ahead. She shook her head and indicated that he should open the box. He did.

There were several stock certificates, a high school diploma, some jewelry and a notebook. Hardy pounced on the book.

"What is it?" Peg asked calmly.

"Nothing. A list of the stocks she has in here." He flicked through the rest of the pages. "That's it." Peg started to close up the box. "Wait a minute," said Hardy. "What's that?"

"Just a piece of paper."

He took out the small yellow document and read it. "How do you like that?"

"What?" asked Peg.

"Eight months ago you were almost an aunt."

"What do you mean?"

"This is a Certificate of Fetal Death. According to Dr. Shapiro, who filled this out, your sister had a premature baby boy who was born dead. Jesus, Peg, I'm sorry. I didn't mean to spit it out like that. I'm sorry, I should have cushioned it a little."

She was leaning against the table, crying. Then she took a deep breath and controlled herself. She was quiet now, but the tears kept streaming.

As Hardy looked at her he felt what he thought was

144

love. He also felt compassion. And frustration at not knowing what to say or do. But, he also felt . . . it was strange . . . her crying made him feel superior, more masculine. She was playing the time-worn woman's role . . . the injured female, dependent on the male. He followed his instincts and took her in his arms and comforted her. He wiped the tears away and cooed to her not to cry. The tears seemed to enhance her loveliness. He wanted her. God, how he wanted her. Her vulnerability increased his desire, but even for him this was not the time. Besides, there was his friend Mr. Pelligrin to worry about. Assuming Peg was right and Dorothy was involved with the Organization. Dorothy had to have been killed because she had something or the Organization thought she had something. Pelligrin might figure, just as Hardy had, that that something was in the safety deposit box. "But it wasn't."

Peg lifted her face from his shoulder. "What?"

"Nothing."

He could tell Pelligrin that they found nothing that would interest the Organization. Of course Pelligrin would believe him. Of course he would.

Peg was still crying. They had to get out of there, and the superior masculine male didn't know what to do. His arm ached. His knee ached. His chest ached. His head ached. He put the death certificate in his pocket and crammed the rest of the stuff into Peg's pocketbook. He gave her his handkerchief. "Blow your nose and fix yourself up. We have to get out of here." He called to the guard. "You can put this away now." They followed the man back to the tier of boxes and watched him put their box back. The man returned Peg's key and took them to the gate and let them out.

"Peg, are you all right?"

"Yes."

"Listen, I don't think we're in for any trouble, but I don't want to take any chances. The first two floors here are part of the bank proper. If someone stands by the staircase he can watch both floors. You go to the third floor which is probably where the offices are. If anyone asks you what you want up there, tell them you're sick and you'd like to use the ladies' room."

"They'll believe that. I must look terrible."

"Stay up there at least five minutes. By that time I'll have led whoever is up there—if there is anyone up there—away from here. Go to your hotel. I'll call you or meet you there. O.K.?"

"O.K."

The elevator was empty. He put her on, rang the third floor and patted her on the behind for luck. As he waited for the elevator to come back, he shook his head at himself. Despite all the trouble he was in or might be in, despite the fear, despite everything that had just happened, all he could think of was the smoothness and the roundness of Peg's ass and how it would be to make it with her.

He looked up to see the guard eyeing him strangely. Hardy pretended to be interested in his nails and examined them until the elevator returned. He pressed two, which would take him to the street level. As an afterthought he pressed one, figuring he could lose any pursuer in the maze of corridors that the first floor level led to.

The face powder and cigar smell was worse than before. It mixed with the smell of his own fear. Hardy thought he would get sick. In that moment between the car stopping and the door opening, a vision of the man without a face flashed before his eyes.

146

The man's voice pounded at his brain. "Tough luck, Fatso . . . tough luck, Fatso . . . tough luck, Fatso." The door opened. No Ben Pelligrin. Feeling relieved and a little silly, Hardy headed for the door. Who was that heading for him? It looked like ice cream face from the boat basin. He had a wild thought that if they killed him in the bank, at least the bank's TV cameras would record it.

Out into the corridor, past the stationers and the passport photo shop. He was heading for the RCA Building. There was a man standing at the foot of the escalator. Hardy didn't recognize him, but he looked formidable and inimical. He doubled back down the stairs and past the hall that led to the post office. Up some more stairs and back the way he came. There was a large crowd using the up escalator. Desperately he ran up the down escalator to the street level. A hand tapped him on the shoulder. All the aches in his body intensified. He turned. A very large man with a very high voice spoke to him.

"Excuse me. Could you tell me where the passport office is?" He pointed vaguely to an up direction and ran out to Fifth Avenue. Saint Patrick's Cathedral loomed before him.

"That's what I need all right. Sanctuary." A bus pulled up. He hopped on, paid his fare and sat down. He closed his eyes and tried not to throw up. In through the nose and out through the mouth. The nausea stopped, and he started to breathe normally. He looked up. Washington Square. He had traveled over fifty blocks in what seemed like seconds.

He was hungry. He trudged over to Macdougal Street and had some Italian sausage, some pizza, some aspirin and some Coke. He walked along Bleecker Street, feeling a little better He belched contentedly and lit a cigarette. He passed a corner phone booth and reminded himself that he should call Peg.

The booth smelled like a urinal, probably because that had been its latest function. Too lazy to find a more pleasant place, he put his dime in and heard it get lost forever in the innards of the phone. He took down the number and started walking again.

As he walked his mind started to function. He knew who killed Dorothy Robbins . . . at least he thought he did. The Organization had nothing to do with it. He had let Peg's fears and suspicions influence him. Probably nobody had been following them. Ben Pelligrin had been in that bank for any number of reasons people go into banks, and not to spy on them. Hardy made a face at his own paranoia and looked around him. Greenwich Village was getting to be more like Coney Island every day. He went into a candy store and bought an egg cream to sip while he used the phone.

"Hi, Peg."

"Oh, Pat, I was so worried. Why didn't you call sooner?"

"I'm sorry. Couldn't be helped. I think I'm onto something. It'll take a little time to work out. You sit tight, and I'll call you back as soon as I can."

"Can't you tell me what it's all about?"

"I'm not sure myself. I'll call you later."

"Pat?"

"Yeah."

"Be careful."

"Always. 'Bye."

He finished his egg cream and walked around until he found a movie house. Lucky day. A double feature.

Three and a half hours later he came out and hailed a cab.

"Where to, mister?"

"Huh?"

"I said, where to?"

He looked up from the yellow document he was examining and gave him Joseph Vanning's address.

Chapter Sixteen

The maid who had answered the door came back and told him that Mr. Vanning didn't care to see him tonight or any other night. Hardy took his notebook out and wrote, "Does your wife know that you are the father of the child that was born dead to Dorothy Robbins eight months ago?" He tore out the page and gave it to the maid.

"Give that to Mr. Vanning, please. I'll wait."

He didn't have to wait long. When he saw Vanning, he backed off a step. The man's anger showed in his face.

"Goddamn you. I ought to kill you. I can't talk to you now. My wife and I have guests coming for dinner. My wife is leaving for the country tonight. I'll call you later."

Hardy reached in his pocket and gave Vanning one of his cards.

"Bon appetit."

As he rode down in the elevator he wondered what

Vanning would do. Suppose he were wrong and Dorothy's death was not a personal thing and was connected with the Organization. Vanning could be calling White right now.

He shook his head and rejected the thought. Vanning wanted that child. He probably blamed the girl for the baby's death and in a rage he killed her ... and in a rage he could kill him. Hardy rubbed his aching arm as that last thought went through his mind. He had really messed up this time. To take his mind off his problems, he did the household shopping he had been neglecting. He went to a delicacy shop on Broadway and got all sorts of cheeses and sausages. Then he went to the liquor store and bought vermouth and another bottle of I.W. Harper.

Tears filled Hardy's eyes. He wiped them with his sleeve and picked up another onion to slice. He wasn't hungry, but cooking helped to take his mind off the matter at hand. On second thought he was getting hungry. Carbonade de bouef a la provencale was one of his best dishes. He put the beef in the marinade and took out the blender in preparation for the creme genois. He had spoken to Peg earlier and told her he would call her tomorrow. He had been tempted to tell her all his suspicions but decided not to. As he went about preparing his meal he tried not to think of Vanning.

The creme was in the refrigerator, and the meat was marinating. He fidgeted for a moment, then decided to fix a broken shelf in the linen closet.

After he finished fixing the shelf, he painted it. When that was done, he washed up and simply sat and waited for Vanning's call. His arm ached a great deal. He took more aspirin and tried to concentrate on a book.

At ten thirty he thought that the beef had marinated long enough. The phone rang as he got up to go into the kitchen.

"Hardy, this is Vanning. Come on up here, you prying son of a bitch, and let's get this thing over with."

He swallowed another couple of aspirins, relieved himself and went to the door. Then back to the bathroom to relieve himself again and out. He started walking downtown. After a few blocks of constantly looking behind, he got on a bus and rode the rest of the way.

Vanning answered the door himself. He was drunk.

"Come on in."

Hardy followed him in, but not too closely.

"I want to warn you, Mr. Vanning. Several people know where I am and if anything happens to me . . ."

Vanning roared with laughter. "What an imagination. What did you think I was going to do? Throw you out the window? You must read a lot of books. Never could stand intellectuals who read a lot of books. How the hell did you ever get into the detective racket? You're no more of a detective than my Aunt Min. I'm not going to kill you. Why should I? I didn't kill Dorothy either. Why should I? I loved her. I'm not going to kill you. I'd like to break your neck, but I won't. So you found out about the baby? I wanted that baby. I was very unhappy when she lost it. Dot wasn't, she was glad. I suppose I couldn't blame her. I don't think she ever believed me when I said I would adopt it. She didn't love me. Just wanted someone around to pay the bills. Tough little kid. Always knew how to take care of number one. She was glad the baby died. She said

152

if it had lived she would have given it away. Some woman in the building . . . Hey! Have a drink."

He poured them both large dollops of Scotch while Hardy sat nervously smoking.

"Last time I saw her was a week after the baby died. That was over six or seven months ago. She said she was through with me. She had been for a long time. Only kept me around to help her out while she was pregnant. After that, it was good-bye, Joe. I never saw her again. I wanted to, but I have my pride. You know who I am? I am Joseph Vanning the fifth. My family helped build this country. People in my family were statesmen and generals. My father was an exceptional man. One of the smartest men on the street. Money. Old money. He left me a lot of it. I spent a lot of it. I am not as smart as my father was about money. My father was a very exceptional man. You know what I am? A flunky. A flunky of the Organization. I wouldn't mind it so much if I were part of the Organization. They happen to be a money-making proposition. I'm just part of their legitimate front. Fine word, 'legitimate.' That's Shakespeare. Didn't know I knew it. I know a lot of things.

"Do you know how much money they take in a day? And from where? From everywhere. Linen supply. Trucking. Kosher meat. Hat check concessions. Records. Unions. Name it. They have a piece of it. Your eyes would pop if you knew how many big firms send an envelope out every week with cold cash in it. And you know where it all ends up? Right. Have another drink."

Hardy drained his Scotch and put out his glass for another. He lit a cigarette from his old one and said nothing.

153

Vanning kept talking. "Fascinating subject. Me and that girl. Only happy thing that ever happened to me was that girl. She wasn't good for me, but she sure made me happy. You want to hear a joke? The place I found her in. The Organization owns that too. Heh. She never knew it, but we both worked for the same boss. She never knew I was with them. Thought I was a rich, respectable businessman. I didn't kill her. You understand me. I didn't kill her."

He had another drink and moved around the room in a drunken pirouette and laughed.

"You know what? If a union member gets a fraudulent insurance settlement they get some of it . . . some of it? Most of it. They own politicians. Unions. Banks. You name it. They have it. Actors, ballplayers, doctors, lawyers, Indian chiefs.

"She was great in bed. Gorgeous body too. I took care of that girl. Gave her a lot of money."

He started laughing again. "You want to hear a joke? I bet the Organization got some of that money too. I gave her, and she gave the Organization their cut. Why not? They have a piece of everything. Want to bribe a politician? They can do it. Hell. They probably put him in office. Want to borrow some money . . . they'll give it to you. And get it back and back and back.

"Do you read all these articles on crime and corruption? They probably own the papers you read them in. I wouldn't be surprised if they were behind some of the riots. There's a profit motive there someplace."

Suddenly he threw his glass at Hardy, who ducked and tensed.

"You ever tell anybody I said any of this, I will kill you. Ah, why bother? Everybody knows anyway.

They just don't want to believe it. You came to find out something. I'll tell you one more time, then I don't ever want to see your ugly, snooping face again. I did not . . . did not kill Dorothy Robbins. If you don't believe me, I don't give a damn. Tell the cops if you want to. I don't care. They're probably part of the Organization too. Everyone is. Even if they aren't . . . Who cares. Get out. Get . . ."

Vanning lurched toward him and fell onto the couch. Hardy swallowed some air and left. When he got home he cooked the bouef provencale, drinking away the hours it took to cook. When it was done, he ate it, threw up and went to bed.

For the first time in a long time he had a pleasant, simple dream. He was a little baby in a cradle and all night long his cradle rocked back and forth and back and forth and back and forth.

In the morning he was hung over, and his arm ached a great deal. The aspirins and coffee seemed to help the hangover, but the arm ache persisted.

He dialed Merle Doyle's number. He heard Chopin and then Merle's voice.

"Hello."

"Hi, it's me, Pat."

"Hello, Pat. I'm glad you called. I have your lab report in front of me."

"Well?"

"Congratulations. You have gout."

"I what?"

"Nothing to worry about. Your uric acid is high. It's a form of arthritis."

"What surprises will you have for me next week? Cancer?"

"Stop feeling sorry for yourself. You're lucky. If it were any other form of arthritis, I couldn't help

155

you. This is treatable. From now on, don't eat liver, brains, kidneys or any other organ foods. Have your druggist call me and I'll give you some pills. Take one every hour, but no more than six today. Then take one tablet three times a day."

Hardy sat and felt sorry for himself for a while, then he called the drugstore.

Later, when he had taken the first pill and the pain in his arm had eased, he called Peg.

"Hi, hon. Look I'm not feeling too well today. I'm going to stay home and take it easy."

"What about the lead you had?"

"It didn't work out. I'm back where I started from. Nowhere."

He hung up and considered what he had just said. He didn't know whether or not he believed Vanning. He just knew he was glad the episode was over and he had gotten through it. As the day went on he took a few more pills and tried to forget his troubles. He did this by reading his latest copies of *Playboy* and *Gourmet*. His arm felt a lot better and he was enjoying himself. He wasn't sure which appealed to him more: the chicken breasts in champagne featured in *Gourmet* or the girl's breasts in bed featured in *Playboy*. As he pondered this the phone rang.

"Hi, stud. Guess who's back in town?"

"Hi, Red. I was just thinking about you."

"I'll bet. Hey. Why don't you come on over?"

"Hey. Why don't I?"

She gave him the address and told him not to dawdle. He shaved and showered and was just starting to get dressed when the first pangs hit him. His stomach was in a knot. He ran into the bathroom and let nature take its course. When he was done he washed the sweat from his face and called Merle.

"Yes, Pat. What's wrong?"

"That's what I'd like to know. All of a sudden I've got the worst case of diarrhea in the history of the world."

"Nothing to get excited about. That's just a side effect of the pill I gave you. Stop taking them today."

He grimaced at the new knot in his stomach. "But what the hell do I do about the 'side effect'?"

"Take Kaopectate. You'll be all right."

After swigging half a bottle, he felt his stomach relax and he finished getting dressed. Holmes barked at him as he went out the door. Halfway to the street he had a touch of 'side effect' and came back. Holmes barked. Hardy did what he had to do and drank a large dose and tried to go out again. As a precautionary measure he stopped by the drugstore and bought another bottle of Kaopectate from the druggist who had made up the pills before. The druggist gave him his package and smiled. "I thought you'd be needing this."

Hardy gave him a dirty look and left the store. He went to the garage to get his car. This was no day to trust to public conveyances.

He paced back and forth waiting for the car, thinking of Ruby's body, and trying not to think of his stomach.

He drove to her apartment, taking little sips from the bottle whenever he could. When it occurred to him that her invitation might be other than what it seemed, he tried to push the thought from his mind. He had been waiting too long to make it with her to let anything stop him. Diarrhea and the Organization notwithstanding, today was going to be the day. He turned on the radio and took another taste of the awful stuff. His stomach felt slightly better.

As he lit a cigarette he heard a newscaster tell about another sniper running rampant in the city.

"My luck he'll plug me just as I'm about to make it." He was there. He parked the car and went up to Ruby's apartment. Outside her door he took a breath and rang the bell.

"It's open."

Hardy went in and closed the door behind him.

"Ruby? Where are you?"

"Is that you, Pat?"

"Yeah."

"I'm in here."

Here was the bathroom. She was in the bathtub. Her wet breasts shone like beacons in a soapy sea. Hardy's stomach relaxed, and the rest of him got excited.

"Don't just stand there," she said laughing. "Come on in." He started to take off his jacket when he noticed the window.

"Don't you ever pull the shades?"

"Let them look. I've got enough." She splashed water at him and made a grab for his crotch. He sidestepped, but not really. He felt himself growing as she held him. Quickly, he turned to pull the shade.

The first shot went past his ear and shattered the tile. His sexual excitement diminished, and he felt his stomach go loose again. Two more shots bounced around the bathroom. Then silence. When he looked up he saw the blood on Ruby's breast.

"Ruby!"

"Relax, lover. I just got nicked by a piece of tile."

He took the washcloth and washed the scratch clean.

"Hey," she said. "That feels good."

"To me too. Let's get out of here first."

158

He helped her out of the tub, and they ran into the living room. They heard more shots which seemed to be coming from across the street. While Ruby dried herself, Hardy dialed 911 and reported what had happened. The police officer told him they already had men at the scene.

Hardy's premonition had been correct. It was the sniper.

The police surrounded and captured the sniper and then came up to Ruby's apartment. The policemen, all strangers, asked them a few questions, asked if Ruby wanted any medical attention, and left.

"Now," said Ruby. "Where were we?"

Hardy's stomach growled a warning at him. "I'm sorry, Ruby, I've got a very important errand I have to attend to. You're going to have to give me a rain check."

Ruby cleared her throat. "O.K., lover. It's your loss. You'd better make it soon though. I might lose interest."

"I'll call you in a couple of days."

He ran out of her apartment and into the nearest movie. All of the facilities were pay toilets and he didn't have any change. Desperately, he crawled under a door, and that was that.

Chapter Seventeen

Friday morning finally came. He had spent a sleepless night. The diarrhea had stopped, but now he was constipated. He forced himself to work out and that made him feel a little better.

As he ate his breakfast, his mind started playing back to him what had happened in the last two days and it kept repeating something that Vanning had said. "Some woman in the building."

"Son of a bitch."

Now he really knew who had killed Dorothy Robbins.

When he rang Mrs. Amanda Delaney's bell, Gerald Friday opened the door.

"Hello, private detective. Congratulations. You figured it out too. You're a busy boy. I heard you got involved with a sniper yesterday. Trouble follows you all the time."

Hardy nodded. "It seems that way. Did she confess?"

"Yep. We're taking her down for a statement now."

Amanda Delaney came out of her bedroom dressed for the street, escorted by another detective and a policewoman. She spoke to her escorts.

"She was a bad person. She didn't keep her promise. That's very rude. I don't like people who are rude to me. I punish them. I punished her." She stared at Hardy.

"What's he doing here? He's rude too. Don't forget to take care of my cats. My babies need someone to take care of them."

Friday nodded to the other detective. "You go along. I want to talk to my friend for a minute. Tell someone to get the ASPCA over here."

After they had gone, Hardy broke the silence. "How'd you figure it out? The baby?"

Friday smiled. "We just found out yesterday. How long have you known?"

"Since Wednesday."

"If you told us you could have saved us a day. A Dr. Shapiro who delivered the baby called us. He'd been in Europe. When he came back he moved into a new house. He saw an old newspaper wrapped around some stuff that had been packed away for him."

Hardy closed his eyes and rubbed them. "Why'd she do it?"

"Why do you think?" Friday asked.

"Dorothy promised her the baby. When the baby was born dead, she blamed Dorothy and killed her."

"That's it."

"Stupid reason. Stupid case."

"They usually are. It's only in books and movies that everything is logical and neat. She killed the dog too."

161

Hardy looked at him. "Huh?"

Friday wiped cat hair from his pants. "She killed the dog—for practice. Then when she was ready, she made a try for Dorothy. That was the mugging report. The crippled doorman saw her and tried to blackmail her. She killed him."

"Didn't you tell me there was another murder? An old woman?"

"Not connected," Friday said. "The nut who did that is probably still out on the street. Just a coincidence that helped to muddle things. Like Larry Leeds and Ginger what's her name. All murders don't tie together."

"I know," said Hardy. "Not like in books and movies. Well, I guess that wraps it up. Looks like Tillie Bushman was smarter than both of us."

"I guess it does. Do me a favor, amateur. Retire. Go into another business. But stay out of mine."

When Hardy got back to his apartment he called Peg and told her what had happened.

"Amanda did it?"

"Yeah, it had nothing to do with the Organization at all. Just a crazy old woman who wanted to be a mother."

Peg made a noise of joy. "And all this time I thought . . . What an idiot I've been. It's all right. Everything's going to be all right."

"Of course it is. This calls for a celebration. Where do you want to go?"

"What's wrong with my place?"

"Nothing at all. I'll see you later."

That night after the room waiter had cleared the dishes, Hardy poured the brandy he had brought with him.

Peg excused herself and said she was going to get comfortable. Nervously, he turned on the TV.

Peg came back wearing Japanese lounging pajamas. She turned off the sound of the television and sat down to drink her brandy. Much to Hardy's annoyance he had to use the bathroom. After washing his hands, he absentmindedly opened the medicine cabinet and moved aside the bottle of dexadrine and took out the diaphragm case. He opened it and was pleased to see that it was empty. Reassured, he went back out to Peg. The room was dark except for the light of the TV. Peg had turned on the radio which was playing endless variations of old-fashioned love songs.

"Hello, darling," she said. "Why don't you come here and rub my neck."

He crossed to her and did what she asked. She cooed and squirmed as he rubbed her neck. His hands moved down to her breasts. Her odors—perfume, sweat, deodorant, brandy and woman—all combined and drew him in. They kissed, and he bit her lower lip which he knew she liked.

He caressed her face. As his fingers touched her lips, she opened her mouth and sucked and nibbled at his fingers. They were like two bursting children. Spring-like, they tightened. She tore off her pajamas and started undressing him. He helped.

"Oh, my God," he said. "You're beautiful."

Even in passion she was vain. She preened at his remark and made her flat stomach flatter and thrust her high breasts higher.

Silently and desperately their lips and hands and bodies explored.

Then little noises from each of them as they fused together, their arms and legs thrashing and propelling

163

them into a sea of ecstasy. He twisted and pounded: a virtuoso pneumatic hammer in an effort to bury himself inside her.

She undulated. A frantic whirlpool drawing him deeper and deeper. The spring grew tighter and tighter—and sprung.

In a passionate vocal ease she screamed her way up the scale and then moaned back down again.

One moment the room had been filled with animal noises; two creatures straining to envelope each other . . . devour each other. Vessels attempting to span hundred-mile gaps . . . take million-mile journeys . . . then silence, except for the sound of their own breathing and shuddering.

Almost immediately they were at it again. This time more frantic than the first.

It was the best he had ever known. It was so good he didn't even want to have his orgasm. He just wanted to screw forever. He was mounted tall in the saddle and riding hellbent for leather . . . laughing all the way.

Again . . . it happened. He felt his soul turn inside out. They didn't separate. Rather they tried to crawl deeper inside each other.

His hand had been grasping her breast. By the light of the silent TV he could see his handprint on her skin. While Sarah Vaughan sang at them, they breathed in their own smells and basked in their own heat. She was sobbing. "Oh. Oh. That was good."

She sobbed some more. He reached over to wipe her tears away. There were none.

He lay there twitching, still inside her. He luxuriated in their oneness. He sighed, as his manhood, almost as an afterthought, sighed with him at being cut down to size, and shrank.

Usually he remembered the specific moments of lovemaking, savoring each good portion . . . a connoisseur . . . this time, no memory . . . Just a feeling of release, relief and contentment.

He took pleasure in the sheer sweat and exhaustion of it all. He smiled contentedly and looked at her. She was smiling too. He leaned over and wiped the perspiration from her face. She opened her eyes and pursed her lips. He kissed her. She grinned happily, said "thank you" and went to sleep.

He drifted off into that quasi-sleep he always slept after sex. His fresh memory of Peg was sweet, but it soon blended with that of Jennifer Burns and what was her name in Paris and so many others . . . and under it all . . . an unidentified memory of something . . . what was it? It didn't matter. He was in that time after sex. A reverie place of things past where one is alone enjoying the aftertaste of pleasure and the memories of former pleasures.

He opened his eyes and watched the Jimmy Stewart-Hedy Lamarr reality run its silent course . . . The sweet horn sound of Bobby Hacket ended, and a man Hardy didn't listen to told the news. He looked back to Peg and admired the lovely blue veins in her breasts as they throbbed. He was disconcerted by the marks her underwear had left on her body and the roughness of her elbows. No matter. The rest of her more than made up for these minor flaws.

The newscaster gave way to Glenn Gould as "Sermonette" presented its silent message on television.

Hardy got dressed, wrote a short note to Peg, kissed her and went home.

At home he had two dishes of creme genois and went to sleep.

In this dream the man without a face was chasing

165

him down a corridor. The walls of the corridor were made of breasts. Hardy tried to hide among the breasts, but they wouldn't envelope him and comfort him. They weren't breasts anymore. They were calluses. Hard, unrelenting calluses. He pounded on them. There was no place to hide.

He woke up, not wanting to open his eyes. If he opened his eyes, he would have to face reality—and he knew what that reality was.

While he had his coffee he made a few phone calls. It was Saturday, and it took time, but he got all the answers he didn't want.

He fingered Peg's key which he had absent-mindedly put in his pocket. Holmes came over, and he scratched him.

"Well, I might as well go and get it over with."

Holmes barked.

"I guess that means you agree with me. I'll be back in a little while. Then we'll go out to the park."

Hardy went directly up to her room without calling from the lobby. He used the key and went in. She was standing nude in the middle of the room. She stared at him in shock.

"Pat!"

"Hello . . . Dorothy."

"Hey, that's pretty good for an amateur." Hardy turned to Ben Pelligrin who was sitting on the couch. He noticed that Ben Pelligrin was wearing only his pants. He also noticed the gun on the couch near his hand. He also wished people would stop calling him an amateur.

She stood there, not trying to cover up. "When did you find out?"

"I realized it this morning. If I wasn't so dumb, I would have known sooner. At least last night when

166

I saw the dexadrine in your medicine cabinet. You were given away by a professional hazard. It sounds silly when you say it out loud. You've got calluses on your elbows. Only bar girls get that from leaning on the bar. There were other things. Those dark glasses you always wore. The way you came on as a nondrinker, then later you proved you weren't. I called your father. He says you never phoned him till the last minute. I don't know who you called that day in my apartment, but it wasn't him. I know, he's a senile old man, but he kept noticing how much more like Dorothy you were than Peg. Then there's the medical examiner. I called him too. The girl who died in your apartment was a virgin. And that's not the Dorothy I know."

The look of shock in her eyes was starting to turn to hate. Hardy wanted to stop talking, but he couldn't.

"I guess my friend Gerald Friday isn't so smart. He now has a victim who was supposed to have had a baby and was a virgin. I guess he'll figure it out."

"Maybe," said Ben Pelligrin. "But too late to do you any good."

Dorothy lit a cigarette. "Don't be so menacing, Ben. All he can prove is that my sister died and not me."

Hardy wanted to try to bluff his way out, but he couldn't stop talking. "Peg's plane did land that night, just the way you said. She came over and the two sisters had a reunion. Check me on this. Here I'm guessing. Peg said something about always wanting to be a blonde but never having the nerve. You said why not, and did her hair right there in the apartment.

Then for some reason, you had to go out. And when you came back you found her dead. You thought the Organization had done it. That's why

167

you were so scared. You covered your own hair or wore a wig and went to the Regal and pretended to be her. Then you dyed it black, and the transition was complete. The haircut was an added touch at changing your appearance. You must have really been rattled to leave so many things in the apartment. Or maybe they weren't important to you. Maybe you took the only real thing of value. The thing you thought the Organization had tried to kill you for."

"That's enough. You talk too much."

"No," said Dorothy. "Let him talk, Ben. I want to hear."

Hardy lit a cigarette. Ben Pelligrin watched his hands as they moved. Hardy took a few drags and wiped the sweat from his brow.

"You must have had a nervous moment when Amanda came into the hall that day at your apartment. What I can't figure is why you ever bothered to come to me about it. You were in the clear with whatever it was you thought they were after. It was all yours. Wait, I get it. You were in it with him. You thought he wanted you dead."

Pelligrin picked up the gun. "Keep talking. You're digging your own grave."

"What do you know?" said Hardy. "A gangster cliché. Friday was wrong again. It is just like the movies. 'Mr. Ben Pelligrin and the cheap stripper had double-crossed the Organization.' What was it? Money? Heroin? A list of names? It doesn't matter. He took it and gave it to you to hold. You thought he double-crossed you. All you wanted me for was revenge. You wanted him to die for trying to kill you."

Dorothy poured herself a drink. "I always knew

168

you were smart, Pat, but so what? What does it all prove?"

"Nothing yet. But your own desires fouled you up. When you were sober you managed to be untouchable Peg. When you drank too much . . . new ball game. That night when I left you, you weren't as drunk as I thought, and you wanted a man. Any man. So you called Larry Leeds. Dumb Larry Leeds. You went over to his place and made love. He was square, wasn't he? He called me to tell me you were alive. You were so afraid of the Organization or Ben here that you killed him to keep him from telling me. That nightmare you spoke about was when you stabbed him to death after having made it with him."

Dorothy filled her glass again. "It's too bad you had to figure that out, Pat. I was going to ask Ben to let you alone. But now I can't do that. Talk about square. I nearly laughed in your face when we first met and you gave me that pitch about sweet little girls from small towns not knowing the score. You New Yorkers are all alike. You think everything happens in the big city. You ought to try a town like East Saint Louis some day. That's where I started. Got a very liberal education too. You were right about what we have though." She picked a suitcase up from the floor and opened it. "See this—five hundred thousand dollars. And it all belongs to Ben and me."

"Was that where you got the money to pay me?"

"Yes. And if you had kept your mouth shut you would have had another ten thousand of it."

"I guess that's it," said Hardy. "Except for one final thing. God, it sure does sound like a movie script. Why was Ginger killed?"

Ben Pelligrin got up and cocked the automatic.

"Not that it matters. That was Organization business. She knew too much about another part of our operation. We used her to go to South America and pick up dope for us. We didn't want you talking to her. You're too nosey for your own good."

"Well, I guess that's another time Gerald Friday was right. Everything doesn't always have to be neat and connecting. My trouble is I was always looking for logical threads to one case, when all along there were three different cases. Who killed her, Ben? Was it you?"

"Your trouble is that you talk too much." He moved the gun toward Hardy.

"No, Ben," Dorothy yelled. "Not here."

"Shut up." He turned back to Hardy. "You were right about her own desires fouling her up. After you left last night she was still horny. I guess you weren't man enough for her. She called me. It shook me up when I found out she was alive. She told me what had happened and that we were just like before. Her and me. Only I changed my mind." He turned to her. "He's right, Baby. You like balling too much. I'd never be sure when you'd dump me for another guy because he had a bigger bulge in his pants than I have."

Hardy knew that Ben Pelligrin was going to kill her.

Suddenly she knew too.

Hardy moved to stop him. Not because of her. He knew he didn't love her. He didn't even like her. He moved because some motor impulse in his brain told him to. Ben Pelligrin raised the gun as his finger tightened on the trigger.

"Tough luck, Baby."

170

Hardy's mind exploded and convulsed in schizoid horror. The film inside his head played again. He watched the man with no face shoot the man in the chair. "No, don't," he screamed. The gun in his brain and the gun in Ben Pelligrin's hand meshed into one. It spat out its deadly message. The man in the chair slumped, his head a bloody mess.

Dorothy screamed and clutched at her beautiful body which now had an ugly red hole in it.

Even as he moved on Ben Pelligrin, Hardy watched Dorothy falling and dying. Even as he watched her dying he thought about her in bed and how good her breasts felt in his hands.

Though his attention was now on Ben Pelligrin, a fraction of him grew sexually excited and recalled Dorothy as she was in bed.

Even in passion she was vain. She preened at his remark and made her flat stomach flatter and thrust her high breasts higher.

It was the best he had ever known.

While the sex memory played on, most of his mind was on Ben Pelligrin.

He saw him here and he saw him in his brain . . . and remembered.

"Tough luck, Baby."

"Tough luck, Fatso."

"Tough luck, Baby."

"Tough luck, Fatso."

Back and forth. Back and forth.

The fear and the hate and the tension of all those years . . . and all those dreams . . . since that day in the barber shop . . . burst out of Hardy and attacked Ben Pelligrin.

Ben Pelligrin couldn't believe his eyes. This maniac

was coming for him. He turned his gun from Dorothy's falling body, finger squeezing as it turned.

Hardy's toe broke Ben Pelligrin's wrist, and the finger stopped squeezing.

Hardy sobbed like a baby while his body, devoid of emotion, methodically did the job of destroying Ben Pelligrin . . . and destroying the man without a face.

Hardy picked up the suitcase and closed it. He dialed 911, told the police where to go, and left the room, taking the suitcase with him.

As he walked along the street, a chauffeured black car cruised along beside him. "Get in, Mr. Hardy." It was White. Hardy got in.

"I believe, Mr. Hardy, that you have my property." White relieved Hardy of the suitcase. "We have been aware of Mr. Pelligrin's duplicity for a long time. You have been a great source of annoyance to me, Mr. Hardy, but you have also done me a great service. Since you are alive, I imagine Mr. Pelligrin is not." Hardy nodded. "As I have said before, you are an amateur, Mr. Hardy, but apparently you are a lucky one. Good-bye, Mr. Hardy. I hope we never meet again."

Fifteen minutes later Hardy picked up his television and watched for an hour. He spent the rest of the day with Holmes in the park. In the evening he went in and ate some cheese and sausage. Then he called Ruby.

"Hi, stud. If you're not here in twenty minutes, I'm going to start without you."

He brushed his teeth and gargled and ran out of the apartment while Holmes barked after him.

This time when Ruby said I'm in here, the here was her bedroom. Hardy looked at her outrageously fantastic form sprawled naked on the bed and forgot everything in the world except her body.

"Come on, stud. I've waited a long time."

Excitedly he crossed to her.

That's when his knee tricked out.

Watch for

Spy and Die
A Patrick Hardy Mystery

Visit

www.speakingvolumes.us

**FIND OUT WHY
THE CRITICS LOVE THE
HISTORICAL MYSTERIES OF
MAAN MEYERS**

Visit us at www.speakingvolumes.us

Award-Winning Author
Annette Meyers

Visit us at www.speakingvolumes.us

Sign up for free and bargain books

Join the Speaking Volumes mailing list

Text

ILOVEBOOKS

to 22828 to get started.

Message and data rates may apply.

FOR MORE EXCITING BOOKS, E-BOOKS, AUDIOBOOKS AND MORE

visit us at
www.speakingvolumes.us

www.ingramcontent.com/pod-product-compliance
Lightning Source LLC
Chambersburg PA
CBHW021459250626
47154CB00004BA/1504